To William

Journey to the Crystal Kingdom

With Love and Best Wishes!

Jk

J.A. Kefford

ISBN-10: 1726322084
ISBN-13: 978-1726322089

DEDICATION

To Paul…my crystal rock!

To Sarah, James and Emily, my three little gems!

To my beautiful grandchildren Mia and Oakley, my magical inspiration!

And to all future generations, Nanna Jaks wrote this especially for you!

ACKNOWLEDGMENTS

Special thanks to my illustrator Sue Hammans-Bayer for her beautiful artwork, which has brought to life the characters in my book and made them even more real to me.

Kirsty Clarke, my talented niece, and editor, who spent many hours making sure my English Grammar was up- to- date and formatting the novel for publication.

Beverly Wolfe, my patient sister, who was my proof reader, and made sense of it all!

Friends of the Waveney Authors Group, and Beccles 'Pen to Paper' Group, who have always been there to offer their wisdom and advice as fellow writers.

Julie Southgate for the crystal reiki sessions, which gave me the self-confidence and belief that I could do this!

Finally, I would like to say a big thank you to all my friends and family for their support and encouragement over the past two years that it has taken to write this novel.

I love you all, and I hope you will enjoy the magic and fantasy I have created for you and your children in the first of the Crystal Kingdom series.

CONTENTS

1. THE DISCOVERY

Mia Ruby was a pretty little girl with big crystal blue eyes and beautiful wavy blond hair, which fell halfway down her back! Her features were petite, but she had very long legs like a giraffe. She was very clever for her age, although sometimes a little argumentative, but she had a sensitive and caring nature, and loved her family dearly.

In contrast, her brother Oakley was smaller in height and stockier in build. His hair was corn coloured and he had big, brown eyes like milk chocolate buttons! Oakley liked to think he was as clever as his sister and would copy her at every opportunity, but he was sportier and more playful. He was very witty too and loved nothing more than to make other children and adults laugh! He was the comedian of the family, and it was very hard to be cross with him. They were both well behaved and adorable children and their Nanny, Nanna Jaks, loved them very much!

Nanna Jaks was a funny old lady with a great sense of humour and a childlike disposition; no one ever believed she was as old as she was. She loved everybody, and everybody loved her! She was always as busy as a bee, flitting from here to there with her big yellow feather duster and singing like Cinderella. She also made the most delicious spaghetti bolognaise and apple crumble.

Both children loved Nanna Jaks as much as she loved them, and they were always keen to stay with her. The little room where they slept at the back of the house facing the garden, was called the 'Fairy Room.' The walls were painted yellow, the white curtains were etched with multi-coloured butterflies and adorning the window sill were lots of fairy ornaments, hence the name of this delightful room.

Nanna Jaks believed in fairies and she was most serious when she said that they lived at the bottom of her garden. Mia and Oakley also believed this, even though they had not seen any. However, they lived in hope that one day they would. When Mummy and Daddy had to go to London for a week, they were very excited because perhaps, during their absence, their wish would come true.

For the first few days, all was as it should be. They helped Nanna Jaks in the kitchen, baking scrumptious cakes and biscuits. When the sun was shining, they helped in the garden with the weeding, although Oakley was more interested in digging up worms, whilst Mia liked to catch tadpoles in Nanna Jaks' pond. In the quietness of the evening, they played cards and board games, and after a cup of hot chocolate, would go upstairs to the Fairy Room where Nanna Jaks read them a story.

On the fifth night of their stay, it was so hot that they both had trouble getting to sleep, and as they lay awake listening to the sounds of the night, Mia heard someone crying in Nanny's garden.

She clambered out of bed to investigate, and as she looked out of the window, to her surprise she could see a bright light shining in the far corner of the garden by the fishpond.

"Oakley! Oakley... come and see this!" she whispered excitedly as she dragged Oakley from his bed to the bedroom window.

Oakley was nearly asleep and more than a little reluctant to follow her, but he rubbed his weary eyes and peered out of the window…"That looks rather strange, hovering and flickering like that! What can it be?" he yawned.

"I don't know…. let's go and find out, cried Mia excitedly…Come on……."

"But I'm tired Mia, and what if it's a UFO? We might be abducted!" Mia thought her brother had such a vivid imagination!

"Don't be so silly Oakley, it is much too small for a UFO" she said sarcastically.

"Oh…you are such a clever clogs" he uttered, his irritation beginning to grow.

"Let's not argue Oakley, we're wasting time…. Let's go and see what it is" she repeated.

"But it's raining!" moaned Oakley, "and we will get wet!"

"Raining… raining?" she queried.

Mia looked out of the window, and in astonishment, saw that it had indeed started to rain, but she wasn't going to be deterred that easily. So, drawing her attention back to her brother, she replied in her grown up and matter of fact manner.

"Don't worry Oakley…Mummy has packed our waterproof jackets and wellies, so we'll just put them on and creep outside without waking anyone up. After all, you must be at least a bit curious?"

When they were both ready, they stepped outside into the dark gloomy night, and headed towards the glowing light at the end of the garden. As they got nearer, the crying they had only faintly heard in the bedroom, grew louder and louder. Then, to their amazement, they saw what was making all the noise...it was a fairy! She was shining as brightly as a beacon, but as the rain fell and she continued to cry, her wings were getting wetter and wetter!

"Oh dear...what is the matter?" asked Mia sympathetically, and so loudly, that the fairy jumped out of her transparent wings and darted behind a garden gnome.

"Don't be afraid" whispered Mia kindly. "We will help you if we can...won't we Oakley?" She turned to her brother, who stood by her side, his mouth agape in wonder! She nudged him, for a reply.

"Sure...we will."

The tearful fairy stepped out from her hiding place, her pretty face alight and now smiling.

"You can see me...you can see me!" she sang, jumping up and down.

"But of course, we can!" said the children in harmony, thinking this fairy was a little crazy!

"Right...introductions first. I am Bluebell, Fairy of Bluebell Glen in the Crystal Kingdom, and I do believe you believe in me, and so I hope you are going to help me."

"How can we possibly do that?" asked Mia, feeling rather confused. Oakley fell silent at his sister's side, allowing her to take charge of the situation.

At this point, the little fairy looked at them and said in a more serious manner "I am so sorry...I am not explaining myself very well. You see, you can see me, and you're awake, which means you really must believe in fairies…in me!"

They nodded their heads in agreement and exclaimed together "Yes, we do believe in fairies! And we will help you if we can!"

"Wonderful!" replied Bluebell, twirling around and around like a spinning top and feeling very dizzy. When she stopped, she fell to the ground in an awkward heap, her hair wetter and more tousled, and her little body gasping for breath. Mia felt very concerned, but before she could say so, Bluebell continued.

"Now I have introduced myself, who am I addressing?"

"I am Mia, and this is my brother Oakley."

"I am pleased to meet you both" declared Bluebell, regaining her composure. She held up her tiny hand to stop any further interruption from the children and proceeded in a more diplomatic tone.

"I have been sent by Queen Cristina to find two children, a boy and a girl, who believe in fairy folk, and will help us save our Kingdom from Queen Matilda, a most wicked fairy who lives and reigns in the Land of Mischief. So, I ask for your confirmation again, do you both believe in fairies?"

"Yes, we do" said Mia and Oakley firmly.

With that, Bluebell waved her magical wand and out of nowhere a glossy piece of paper and a white feather quill fell into her small tiny hands.

"Now all I need is your signature to swear allegiance to Queen Cristina, and the fairy folk of the Crystal Kingdom."

She then handed Mia this document.

"Wait a minute! I'm just a little bit afraid and worried about what Oakley and I am expected to do...after all, we have no magical powers. And why is this fairy threatening your realm? Is she not happy where she lives?"

Mia and Oakley believed all arguments could be settled peacefully if people just talked and worked out their grievances; surely it would be the same for fairies?

Bluebell looked at Mia, and understood her confusion and apprehension, because she was so young. But without the help of these two special children, the light of the good fairies would grow dim, and the hopes and beliefs of future kingdoms would be no more! She did not want to frighten them, so she politely requested "Please let us go inside, and we will discuss the matter further. I am rather cold out here and my wings are so wet, I need to dry them off, before I can fly home."

"Okay…" said Mia. "Follow us, and don't make too much noise otherwise you will wake Nanna Jaks."

Then she walked ahead with Oakley two steps behind her, but as she reached the back door and turned to usher Bluebell in, Bluebell had vanished.

2. THE CLUE

After the disappearance of Bluebell, Mia and Oakley went back to their beds feeling very disappointed and upset that their new acquaintance hadn't stayed longer. They didn't understand what had frightened her away and were rather concerned that she couldn't fly because of her wet wings.
It had been a long night, and soon they were fast asleep, forgetting Bluebell and her plight.

The following morning, they awoke to the birds singing happily outside their bedroom window. The sun shining brightly, with the haze of a beautiful rainbow forming in the sky above.

Oakley was the first to comment on their discovery in the garden the previous night. "Mia…Was Bluebell really here, or did we dream it all?"

"Don't be silly Oakley, I saw her too you know, so how can we both have dreamed it?"

"Do you think she'll come back? Oakley asked tentatively.

"Well, she said she needed our help, and we didn't say no" declared Mia thoughtfully.

"Yeah….but we didn't sign her piece of paper either" replied Oakley.

"I know, but I am sure Bluebell wouldn't give up on us that quickly. Let's just wait and see what happens!"

The two children proceeded to get washed and dressed, forgetting the little fairy for the time being, and with their stomachs now rumbling with hunger, all they could think of was Nanna Jaks' hearty breakfast awaiting them downstairs.

Nanna Jaks was, as usual, cheerily singing when they entered the kitchen.

"Did you sleep well, my little darlings?" she smiled.

Mia and Oakley nodded in unison.

"Scrambled eggs, bacon and beans, followed by warm pancakes and maple syrup, just for you two!" she chirped with an Irish lilt.

Before they could answer or protest, she beckoned them to the table. "Now sit down and eat it *all* up!" she joked… "And when you're both finished, I think we'll all have some fun in the garden today."

Oakley was just about to confide in Nanna Jaks, when Mia looked at him; with a quick wink of her eye and a finger to her lips, he knew he was not to say a word about the events of last night! He loved keeping secrets, so his sister didn't have to worry about him telling anything!

After they'd finished their delicious breakfast, Nanna Jaks told them to go and play outside while she cleared the dishes away. So alone, they decided to revisit the spot in the garden where they had found Bluebell crying. They sat on the bench near the pond and scanned around them to see if there was any evidence of the little fairy.

"Come on Oakley...I am sure Bluebell has left us some clue, after all, the tooth fairy always leaves magical dust and a silver coin under the pillow."

"Oh Mia, you're so clever! Of course, why didn't I think of that?" said Oakley enthusiastically, and with that he jumped up off the bench and started to search around him. Mia did the same!

At this point, Nanny came out into the garden with her weeding tools. She called to them both, for she knew they liked to help her. She was very educated in plants and flowers and tended her garden with great care and devotion. Mia especially loved to know the names of flowers, as lots of her friends were called after them!

She handed Mia and Oakley a small trowel and bucket each and pointed out the patch of garden she would like them to weed.

"Now, children, I have just put some new flowers in that bed, so I will point them out to you, so you don't mistake them for weeds. Here we have geraniums, marigolds, petunias and... bluebells."

"Bluebells!" exclaimed Mia, coughing and spluttering.

"Yes, my dear, just in front of that garden gnome. Are you alright?" Mia had gone bright red, which usually happened when she had something to hide, but Nanny didn't seem to notice.
As Nanny walked away, Mia couldn't contain her excitement any longer.

"That's it Oakley! Perhaps what we need to find is buried within the bluebells...we will just have to be very careful we don't damage them, otherwise Nanny will be upset!"

As they lifted the bluebells delicately from the earth, sure enough, the white feather quill and glossy paper lay beneath, and with them, a small blue crystal.

"You were right Mia, but what do we do now?" asked Oakley in puzzlement.

"I think we should read it again, and then if we are happy to help, we sign it" said Mia triumphantly.

Looking closely over his sister's shoulder, Oakley exclaimed "But there is nothing to read, it's just a blank piece of paper!"

Mia agreed, but then this wasn't an ordinary piece of paper, it was magical. It could be written in invisible ink, or perhaps the writing was too small for the human eye.

Oakley was becoming impatient and tried to snatch the crystal, which Mia had just picked up.

"Wait a minute Oakley. Let me look at it first!" Mia examined the crystal more closely, her mind racing. "It could be that the crystal acts like a magnifying glass to read the document," she explained to her brother.

"Mia…you're so brainy!" he declared, smiling proudly and exposing his shiny white, even teeth.

To avoid arousing Nanny's suspicion, they decided to wait until bedtime to read closely through the document. If they were totally sure of the conditions, and indeed brave enough to help save the Crystal Kingdom, then they would sign their allegiance.

3. THE ADVENTURE BEGINS

Mia and Oakley couldn't wait to go to bed to read the *fairy* letter! Nanna Jaks was most surprised when they both announced they wanted to go to their room at 7 o'clock, when the sun was still shining and even more so, when they didn't want a bedtime story!

They raced up the stairs, washed and changed into their pyjamas, then called Nanna Jaks for a goodnight kiss.

"Goodnight my sweethearts, sleep tight and don't let the bed bugs bite; if they do, I'll come and save you" she laughed wholeheartedly.

"Not if we save you first!" they giggled. Nanny gave them the biggest kiss and cuddle, as she always did, and left the room.

No sooner had she gone, both were on their feet. The tiny piece of *fairy* paper, which had been hidden under Oakley's pillow, along with the feather quill pen and blue crystal, were taken out. As usual, Mia took charge.

"Oakley, please put the paper down on the bedside table and hold the crystal over the top. Now move it from side to side." she instructed.

"Okay" agreed Oakley, feeling very useful at last. As Mia was very good at reading, she could decipher the message easily, which verified all that Bluebell had said and more. Finally, she read out aloud the declaration that they would honour and protect Queen Cristina and the Crystal Kingdom. She looked at her brother for confirmation, and he nodded his head in agreement. They then both signed their consent with the magical quill.

At once, the little piece of paper rose into the air, whirled around their heads, before disappearing; a cascade of magical fairy dust followed. The children were mesmerised, and the silence in the room was palpable.

"Wow!" they exclaimed, becoming rather excited.

"What next?" queried Oakley, rather impatiently.

"I don't know…" said Mia. "Perhaps we have to do something more."

"Like what?" asked Oakley, feeling a little disappointed that the 'magic show' had ended.

"I think we need to find Bluebell, or maybe call for her" replied Mia with exasperation. "She will know what to do next!"

"Bluebell...Bluebell...Where are you?" shouted her brother loudly.

"Sshh……Nanny will hear you" whispered Mia.

Suddenly, they heard a tiny little voice echoing from the bedside table. They both ran in the same direction, nearly colliding with one another in their excitement to investigate further.

"We can hear you, but we cannot see you" they chorused.

"Look in the crystal" directed Bluebell, speaking as loudly as she could.

The children turned their attention to the crystal, which was now glowing brightly. Mia was the first to pick it up. Looking deep inside its core, she could just see Bluebell, with her butterfly-shaped wings and golden wavy hair, delicately clipped back with the flowers of her namesake. She looked so beautiful and so different from the wet and bedraggled fairy they had met the previous night.

"Oh! gasped Mia. "This is rather strange…what are you doing in there?"

"If you wish me out, I can explain everything" answered Bluebell.

Oakley stood at his sister's side, staring in bewilderment at the talking crystal, and on hearing Bluebell's command, he said impatiently "Come on then, I WISH YOU OUT!"

Immediately, there was a small explosion, as though a firework had been set-off. A scattering of brightly coloured stars lit up the room, and there appeared Bluebell on the bed.

"What an entrance!" cried out Oakley, not quite believing his eyes.

"Why, thank you very much" replied Bluebell in appreciation. "Now you know where I live, you must understand that rule number one is, if you are in trouble, I will not be far away if you need me. So *please* keep my crystal in a very safe place and *never* let it out of your sight!"

"Rules, rules" uttered Mia. "I hate rules. It's always the same, do this, do that, or you will be in trouble!" Oakley agreed with his sister, but he kept quiet.

"Now now" hushed Bluebell, rules are set for your own safety, and it is very important you take note, if we are to succeed in

saving the kingdom. Mia fell into silence and lowered her head feeling ashamed.

"And we also have no time to feel sorry for ourselves, so apology accepted, let's move on" added Bluebell abruptly.

"It is time for the adventure to begin. Mia, I want you to pick up the feather quill and twirl it above and around your head" she ordered, in a gentle manner.

With Oakley standing closely by her side, Mia circled the pen in the air above, making a slight breeze in the room. Lots of tiny white feathers began to fall like raindrops. Both children stared in wonder as the feathers started to gather in the formation of a beautiful white swan.

"Cool" cried Oakley.

"Amazing" declared Mia.

The swan was very elegant and very proud, and she looked at the children lovingly.

"Right" interrupted Bluebell. "This is Serena, she will be flying us to the Crystal Kingdom. But before we leave, I must ask you to drink your bedtime milk and eat the cookies that Nanna Jaks has left for you on your bedside table. We have a long journey ahead of us and I don't want you to get hungry!"

Mia and Oakley didn't recall Nanna Jaks bringing these nightcaps up, but sure enough there they were on the table as Bluebell had said, so they both obeyed the little fairy, without further question.

Instantly, the room around them seemed to grow bigger and bigger! In shock, they turned to Bluebell, who they were now equal in size to. The swan however, was the largest of them all!

"It's alright" reassured Bluebell, "It is necessary that you are as small as me and all the fairy folk, so you are not mistaken for giants when we get to the Crystal Kingdom, otherwise there will be sheer panic in the land, and we don't want that, do we?"

"Why, of course not!" they both acknowledged.

Bluebell then beckoned them forward towards Serena, who now lay with her wing outstretched on the floor for them to climb upon. As they all walked along it, they saw, buried amongst the white feathers of her back, Bluebell's crystal, and a small doorway leading into the heart of it. The three entered, and to the children's astonishment, they found themselves in a small room identical to their bedroom at Nanna Jaks, which surely, they had just left!

They turned to Bluebell, looking for an answer, but Bluebell just winked and giggled, and with a finger to her lips she said "Sshh now children, it is time for bed. Explanations tomorrow…. Goodnight." Before they could utter one word of complaint, both were fast asleep!

4. HIGHWAY TO THE STARS

The following morning, Mia and Oakley awoke to the smell of hot porridge. It tickled their taste buds and they were only too eager to get out of bed and have some! As they walked through the crystal door, they found themselves in another room. Bluebell was sitting at a table with a little old fairy who had twinkling crystal blue eyes and wispy pink hair like candy floss. Although she looked old with her wrinkly face and wings, she was still very beautiful. Upon seeing the children, she jumped up from her chair, grabbed the pot of porridge from the stove and began dishing it up into four bowls. She beckoned them over.

"Okay my dears, sit yourselves down and eat up, before it goes cold!" she advised, darting here and there but managing to arrange the breakfast table in an orderly fashion. Mia and Oakley were amazed at her nimbleness and efficiency; she was just like Mary Poppins!

"Are you related to Mary Poppins?" asked Mia, thinking out aloud.

The old fairy burst out laughing, 'No my dear, I'm much older and wiser than her… I'm Twinkle!"

"Twinkle who?" queried Oakley.

"Twinkle, fairy of the stars" she replied proudly.

"Of course!" guessed Mia… "Twinkle Twinkle little star" and she started to sing the well-known nursery rhyme, with Oakley deciding to join in half way through.

"Why thank you so much, that was lovely!" Twinkle smiled affectionately at both children and clapped her hands in appreciation.

"Now please come and eat your porridge and drink your orange juice, and then after we have all finished, we will discuss how I am able to help you in your mission."

Throughout breakfast, Mia and Oakley were very quiet, enjoying their porridge too much to think of anything else. When they had finished, Twinkle led them from her kitchen into another room, but before they went in she handed them a special pair of dark glasses.

"Put these on please, they will protect your eyes" she instructed. The children obeyed Twinkle and followed her into the room. At first, both were speechless, until Mia broke the silence.

"Oh...this is spectacular!" she exclaimed.

"Spec....tac...u... lar" repeated Oakley, a bit unsure of how to pronounce the word, but attempting it anyway.

"It's so beautiful!" added Mia.

"So awesome!" replied Oakley.

The ceiling, walls and floor space was filled with millions of stars, shining so radiantly they illuminated the small room with a golden glow. Mia and Oakley felt like they were floating in the sky itself.

"These are 'my children'" said Twinkle tenderly. "I look after each and every one of them during the daytime, and at night time I scatter them throughout the sky to shine through the dark on your planet Earth."

"How incredible!" gasped Mia and Oakley in unison.

"Right my dear children, I have a gift to give you, which will help you in your quest!"

Taking her fairy walking stick, which appeared from nowhere, she pointed to the stars above and wished a handful of them to fill a small velvet purse held out in her free hand. The stars, so pretty and bright, fell like miniature shooting stars into the purse, which she then gave to the children. Mia and Oakley felt very excited, and thanked Twinkle.

"But what do we do with them?" asked Oakley, looking at Twinkle for an answer. "After all, they belong in the sky" he stated.

Mia glared at her brother, and said in a most grown up fashion, "Don't be so impatient Oakley! I'm sure Twinkle will tell us how to use them. Just give her a chance."

Twinkle looked at Bluebell, who had just joined them; both fairies smiled. They knew there were many things to explain to the two children.

"All will become crystal clear as the adventure unfolds, but I think it is time for a fairy story" beamed Twinkle lovingly. "Let's go back to the kitchen and I'll make you a cup of my delicious hot chocolate. Then, you must return to Bluebell's

crystal and settle down for the night. You have a long day ahead tomorrow."

"It can't be bedtime" said both children reluctantly.
"We've only just had breakfast!" moaned Oakley.

"Time always flies when you're having fun" replied Bluebell, and as they all walked out of the Star Room, she winked at Tick Tock, a little pixie holding a watch-like wand in the corner of the room. The children hadn't noticed him.

"Come on children, your hot chocolate is going cold!" Twinkle shouted from the kitchen.

Mia and Oakley looked at one another in surprise.

"Bluebell…How does she do that?" asked Mia.
"Yeah…she moves so quick for such an old fairy!" giggled Oakley.

Bluebell said nothing, but just laughed.

After they drank their hot chocolate, they returned to the crystal house, and got into bed. Twinkle soon appeared with her storybook in hand, and settled herself in the rocking chair, with Bluebell sitting at the foot of Mia's bed.

"Are we all comfortable?" chuckled Twinkle. Everyone nodded.
"Right, I am going to start from the very beginning....

Once upon a time, two twin girls were born to the King and Queen of the Crystal Kingdom. They were beautiful princesses. Cristina's hair was golden, Matilda's was ebony.

28

But although both were beautiful, Matilda was not as kind and loving as Cristina; she was always causing trouble. Matilda bullied and teased the fairies, so was greatly disliked by them. However, Cristina loved the fairies as much as she loved her sister, and was protective of the crystals they lived in. No one could understand the reason why they were so different!

When the princesses reached their 18th birthday, it was to be decided who would rule the Crystal Kingdom and who would rule the Land of Make Believe, both magical kingdoms. This should have been a very difficult choice to make, but because of Matilda's attitude, it was proclaimed that she would reign over the Land of Make Believe.
It was a land just as beautiful as the Crystal Kingdom, with friendly gnomes, dwarves, pixies, and even dragons and giants, but no crystal fairies resided there; that was the law. The King and Queen believed that this was best for their daughter, but Matilda hated the fairies even more, and blamed them for losing her childhood home and family.

Over the years, she allowed her subjects to do as they pleased, ignoring all their complaints, troubles and naughtiness. She also delighted in renaming the kingdom, The Land of Mischief.

With darkness and gloom gradually spreading across her land, Matilda has begun to steal the crystals from her sister's kingdom, hoping to restore the light to her own, and enslaving the fairy who lives within. But little does she know that it is her own wickedness that has caused the darkness to prevail.

"I don't understand" interrupted Mia. "Why couldn't the fairies stop her?"

"Yeah" said Oakley. "After all, they have magical powers."

"If only matters were so simple" sighed Bluebell.

"She is a queen, and fairies cannot be disloyal" Twinkle reminded her. "That is why, we need your help. Queen Matilda and her subjects are unable to enter the Crystal Kingdom, so she has persuaded children like yourselves to steal the crystals for her."

"Then, surely, you can talk to these children and tell them what is going on?" replied Mia.

"It is not as easy as that" stated Twinkle.

"Why not?" asked Oakley.

"Because, they are under her spell, which only you two children can break" emphasised Twinkle.

"So, we have got to find and rescue the crystal fairies, break a spell on some children we don't even know, and face the anger of Queen Matilda?" said Mia apprehensively.

"Ohhh…That sounds difficult *and* really scary!" added Oakley, beginning to feel rather nervous.

"Don't worry children, you already have my gift, the purse full of magical stars" reassured Twinkle.

"And what will they do?" queried Mia, trying not to sound too ungrateful.

"Well, my dear, they will guide you safely through the Land of Mischief, because as I have said, it's a very dark and gloomy place. My stars will light the way to the castle where we believe the fairies and bewitched children are being held."

Twinkle knew the quest ahead was going to be difficult, but she hoped her answer would allay their fears for the time being.

Suddenly, Mia and Oakley felt very sleepy. It had been such an exciting day, and as Twinkle began to rock gently back and forth in her chair, singing them her own lullaby, they were soon fast asleep.

"Goodnight, goodbye and good luck" said Twinkle, as she kissed them both fondly on their cheeks.

As she stepped out of the crystal house, she issued Bluebell a smile and waved her hand before disappearing into her own cosy starlit room.

5. BUBBLES TO THE RESCUE

When Mia and Oakley awoke the following morning, they remembered everything Twinkle had said to them, and were eager to see her again to thank her for their lovely day and the gift she had given them. They quickly got dressed and stepped outside into the warm sunshine, but Bluebell and Twinkle were nowhere to be seen.

As the children looked around, they realised they were in a different place; it was like a rainbow had fallen out of the sky and everything had been painted in vivid colours!

"Red and yellow and pink and green...orange and purple and blue" sang Mia happily. Oakley joined in, when suddenly Bluebell appeared smiling. Behind her followed a beautiful white unicorn, pretty butterflies chasing one another, a swarm of ladybirds, and a colourful cockatoo.

Mia stopped singing abruptly and turned her attention to Bluebell and the strange party.

"Where are we?" she asked.

"And who are your friends?" Oakley interrupted.

"Well I see you are both up early and ready to leave, so I'll explain." Bluebell waved her wand and a large map appeared before her.
"We have arrived in Rainbow City" she pointed on the map, "and you will be heading south towards the Crystal Kingdom. To the north, lies the Land of Mischief. There should be no danger on this journey, but we are not going to take any

chances, so the ladybirds will fly ahead to make sure everything is fine, and the butterflies will form a canopy around you, to shelter you from the heat of the sun, but *most* of all, to protect you from being seen. The unicorn will carry you, and she can move swiftly if need be. And Charlie the cockatoo, is your royal chaperone."

"That's right mateys! I'm the guvnor 'round here, so no one will argue with me, unless they want some fisticuffs. I've been appointed by her maj!" he proclaimed in his London cockney accent.

"And I am Lightning, light on my feet and gone in a flash!" said the unicorn jokingly.

Both children giggled, and thought the journey was going to be such fun with their new friends!

Bluebell couldn't stay as she was needed at the palace, but she left her crystal with them and said they were to keep it safe, and only wish for her if they were in extreme danger.

"Goodbye children, I will see you soon at the palace. Until then, please take care and do what Charlie tells you."

"We will" promised Mia and Oakley.

"Hey kids, are you hungry?" asked Charlie. "How about some kippers? I'm a pretty good catch if I say so myself!"

"Perhaps you would prefer some fruit... apples are my favourite!" added Lightning.

"Fish and apples for breakfast!" protested Oakley. "That's disgusting!"

"Not if you're hungry" chuckled Charlie and Lightning.

Mia and Oakley had to agree, but to avoid offending anyone, they decided to eat the apples for breakfast, and save the fish for later.

As they travelled through the multi-coloured fields in the summer sunshine, the ladybirds flitted back and forth, reporting traffic and weather problems ahead, whilst Charlie read the map and diverted the journey where necessary. Lightning plodded on slowly and the children soon fell asleep on her back, feeling safe and comfortable under the shade of the butterflies overhead.

A few hours later, Mia and Oakley awoke feeling rather hungry. They sat up and Mia called to Charlie, "Do you think we could stop and eat those kippers now?"

"Well…eh… of course …but um I …." Charlie stammered.

"Oh, you are a silly parrot" teased Oakley.

"Don't be so rude Oakley!" reprimanded Mia.

"Yeah....don't call me a parrot" exclaimed Charlie, "I'm a cockatoo!"

The children looked at one another and began to laugh.

"Right that's it! I think we'll all go and catch some fresh fish" ordered Charlie. "I don't want you two getting upset stomachs from eating ol' kippers." The truth was that he'd already eaten them while they were sleeping but didn't want to admit it.

Mia and Oakley loved to go crabbing with their parents, so they were very excited about going fishing and ran after Charlie, as he flew ahead leading the way to a small stream nearby. They watched as he dived in and out of the water catching the fish with ease. They decided to make a couple of fishing rods out of small sturdy branches, the laces from Oakley's shoes, and a couple of dead worms. But as they paddled in the stream and cast their lines, they weren't as lucky as Charlie, and soon became bored, so Oakley started trying to jump across the stepping stones which made a path across the stream.

"Oakley...don't do that" called Mia anxiously. Charlie was too busy to notice what was going on, and a little too far away, so Mia felt she was now in charge of her younger brother.

"Stop Oakley! You will slip and fall in..." she began to shout, becoming more concerned than ever.

"It's fun Mia...you try it!" he yelled back excitedly.

"No...it's dangerous!" she bellowed.

Suddenly, there was an almighty splash. Oakley had lost his footing and fallen into the water. Without thinking Mia dived in, after all she was a good swimmer, but the current was stronger, and it dragged her down. In front of her she saw Oakley being pulled under too. Desperately, she reached for his outstretched hand and with the other hand, withdrew the tiny crystal stored in her pocket and summoned Bluebell to

help them. Instantly, the water around them became a mass of bubbles; immersed in the bubbles was a fairy, but not Bluebell!

"Hubble Bubble, one two three, you're as safe as you can be" chanted the pretty fairy.

Next minute, both children were encapsulated in one of the bubbles, which floated to the top of the stream and carried them safely to the water's edge. As it touched the grassy bank, it popped, and they stepped out!

"Cor *blimey*!" gasped Charlie guiltily, seeing what had happened at the last minute and flying over to them. "I thought I'd lost the pair of you!"

"Oh Bubbles, Bubbles...how can I thank you enough?" He turned to the little fairy, who sat unnoticed by the children on a grassy knoll.

"Yes, thank you," said Mia kindly, turning her head in the direction to where she could now see Bubbles more clearly. She was so pretty with her cherubic face, red curly hair and green eyes, but more outstanding were her fine, beautiful fin-like wings of aqua blue.

"Without your help, we would have drowned," declared Oakley, being more grown up and serious than Mia had ever known him to be.

"It is no trouble at all," sang Bubbles. "Any friend of Bluebell's is a friend of mine!" Then with a loud pop and a shower of tiny bubbles, she disappeared!

"Come on children, let's get you back to the campsite, and dried off. I don't want you both catching a cold. If this gets back to the palace, I could end up as parrot pie!" he cried, a look of fear etched on his face.

"Don't worry Charlie, it wasn't *really* your fault," Mia sympathised.

She was beginning to love this quirky little bird and she didn't like to think he would get into any sort of trouble.

"Anyway, you can't end up as parrot pie, because you're a cockatoo!" she reminded him, and they all burst into fits of laughter.

****

When they reunited with Lightning and the rest of the party, Charlie immediately prepared a campfire, so they could get warm and dry again. He was very quiet as he cooked the fish he had caught from the stream, reflecting on the seriousness of what had happened. While Charlie was busy, the children told the unicorn of their lucky escape and how Bubbles had rescued them.

The fish was delicious and with full stomachs and the setting sun, Mia and Oakley began to yawn, so Lightning suggested they come and settle by her. As they nestled down in the warmth and comfort of her fluffy white mane, they were soon fast asleep, dreaming of the next day's adventure.

6. McDUFFUS' FARM

The following day, the children awoke to the sound of thunder in the distance. It had started to rain, and they noticed that the butterflies had disappeared, and the ladybirds, with their metallic red and black spotted wings, had formed an umbrella above their heads. Charlie sat proudly on the top of Lightning's alicorn, looking through a pair of oversized binoculars, checking the road ahead.

"This is not good…not good at all!" he mumbled to himself.

"What's wrong Charlie?" said Mia uneasily.

"Oh! You're awake miss! It would seem we have run into some lousy weather and we are going to have to make a detour, as the field adjacent to McDuffus' farm is waterlogged, which means we will now have to pass through the *old* farmer's land."

"Surely, that can't be too much of a problem; we can just politely explain our situation, and ask his permission to cross" exclaimed Mia, trying to be helpful.

"I wish it was as simple as that" replied Charlie nervously, "but McDuffus' land belongs to Queen Matilda and she has her spies everywhere."

At the mention of the evil fairy's name, both children visibly shook and fell into silence.

"Then, what are we going to do?" asked Oakley, speaking up and fearing for the safety of them all.

40

"There is no other way, we will have to take our chances" explained Charlie with conviction. "And anyway, seeing both of you will at least give some hope to McDuffus."

"Can we trust the farmer then?" Oakley queried, still feeling worried.

"Yes...absolutely" stated Charlie, and he began to tell the story about poor old McDuffus, who had a flourishing farm years ago. "His family, workers and animals were all so happy, but when Matilda became Queen of the Land of Make Believe, she took everything from him, so he had become very bitter and resentful. He was made to supply the castle with fruit from his orchards, wheat and grain, and livestock. Now, he no longer has anything but the roof above his head and a few faithful friends. Even his wife and children were taken to the castle to serve the Queen."

When Charlie had finished, Mia and Oakley felt sorry for McDuffus.

"We must help him!" declared Mia, "but what if Matilda is watching, or worse still, *hiding* on the farm and waiting to capture us?"

Charlie didn't know what to say, for although Mia was young, she was very smart, and she could be right about Matilda either way, but Charlie hoped and prayed it was the former option.

"I'm counting my cockatoos that she's watching us and getting her knickers in a twist with fear of your arrival!" he joked, trying to make light of the situation, which did the trick as both children began to giggle.

Finally, the decision made, they entered the gate leading into McDuffus' field. No sooner had they done so, it was as though all alarm bells had been activated. Firstly, a cow with a huge bell around her neck came charging towards them, followed by a pig snorting madly and a dog barking loudly. There was also something else, too small to be seen, but squeaking shrilly. As they all surged forward, kicking up a cloud of dust, nobody saw the huge tractor coming from behind, until they were practically surrounded and there was silence and visibility once more.

Mia, Oakley, and even Charlie, had buried their heads deep in Lightning's mane, and now all three popped up to speak with their assailants.

"Hello..." said Mia meekly.

"We come in peace" stated Oakley diplomatically, and he withdrew a handkerchief out of his pocket and waved it bravely in the air; but to his surprise, it wasn't his handkerchief, but the magical contract he and Mia had signed.

Swiftly, it was snatched from him, by a little old dwarf with a long white beard and spectacles, who seemed to have appeared from nowhere.

"Give that back!" shouted Oakley.

"Get your hands off her majesty's private correspondence!" squawked Charlie, beginning to flap about. The dwarf examined all of them over his spectacles, frowning... "Just stay where you are and be quiet!" he commanded.

Instantly, they were all speechless and frozen to the spot. Charlie looked very funny in mid-air suspension. Even Lightning did not move! The old dwarf looked closely at the piece of paper and when he spoke, the spell was broken.

"Good day to you wee bairns. I am McDuffus and I welcome you" he said in his Scottish accent. "This is my dear old friend Jack" he pointed to the dog at his side, "Libby, my beautiful milk maiden, Penelope my housekeeper and Pipsqueak, my very own pixie protection."

"A housekeeper for a pig!" laughed Oakley, forgetting his manners.

"You may live in a sty, young sir, but I do not!" protested Penelope in a most posh manner.

"And before you insult *me* young man, I am a milk maiden and *not* a cow!" said Libby, even more arrogantly.

Oakley looked at Mia and just chuckled.

McDuffus continued. "I am sorry that I startled you children, but I had to convince Matilda that I was trying to capture you. She sees everything through her crystal mirror. But with Tick Tock here, to stop time, you will be able to pass through this field safely."

"Tick Tock!" exclaimed Mia and Oakley.

"Who is he?" asked Mia, with curiosity.

"More to the point, where is he?" queried Oakley.

"Here!" yelled Tick Tock, darting in front of them. The children stood in awe of this funny little pixie with the wheels of time etched on his wings, and an hourglass necklace. He also held a wand, much taller than he, with a small watch on the tip.

"No time for dilly dallying!" interrupted Charlie, who was eager to move on, knowing Matilda could appear any minute.

"Quite right, hurry up all of you, you're wasting my time!" teased Tick Tock.

"Please Tick Tock, one more minute. I need a favour…" said McDuffus expectantly.

"Time doesn't stand still!" Tick Tock joked again.

McDuffus turned to Charlie and the children and explained that Pipsqueak needed to return to the Crystal Kingdom, as it was no longer safe for him to stay at the farm. Matilda would now be aware of his presence and take him to the castle as her prisoner once she arrived.

"But what about yourself Mr. McDuffus?" asked Mia, with great concern. "Surely Matilda will realise that you have fooled her, and will hold you captive too?"

"It's alright Mia, I will be fine. I am an old dwarf and Pipsqueak has protected me over the years whilst keeping Queen Cristina informed of her sister's activities. But it is time to say farewell to him" he said bravely.

"Time to go! Time to go!" shouted Tick Tock, flitting around everybody.

"Okay Tick Tock, patience is a virtue…" mocked Charlie.

Pipsqueak and McDuffus embraced one another, then Tick Tock whispered in the old dwarf's ear... "You will remember nothing that has happened in the last hour, as time stands still."

As Lightning carried Pipsqueak and the children on her back across the field, Charlie kept watch from high above. Below, he saw McDuffus, Jack, Libby and Penelope stood frozen in time, awaiting the arrival of Queen Matilda.

7. WHISPERING WOODS

After the excitement of the day, Mia and Oakley felt exhausted. Pipsqueak whistled a happy, but rather squeaky, tune in their ears; the hypnotic melody soon lulled them to sleep, as they snuggled down in Lightning's deep, soft and silky mane. Charlie kept a mindful eye on the road ahead, and the umbrella of butterflies returned to protect them from the heat of the sun.

****

Back on McDuffus' farm, Queen Matilda had arrived with her army of gnomes, led by Grimball, and she was furious that the children had escaped her clutches.

"Grimball, what have you to report?!" she demanded in exasperation.

"Well Ma'am, it's like this" he stammered. He bowed his head in shame, knowing he had failed her. The sudden silence was ominous, as he waited for her temper to boil over and the torrent of angry words to begin.

"Look up you stupid gnome and tell me why we haven't succeeded in our plans! After all, I can see from my magic crystal mirror, there is only a *small* party protecting these children, and with your *large* army Grimball, it should have been an easy task to capture them!" she shouted.

"Well…your majesty…it would appear that … erm…urgh" he stuttered again.

"Oh, shut up Grimball! You have no excuses, you blithering idiot! Bring me McDuffus, at least *he* may know in which direction they went to the Crystal Kingdom. It would also seem that he has been protecting a pixie, an agent of P.L.U.M (Pixie Liberation Underground Movement) who may have discussed details of my sister's mission against me" she said eagerly.

"Wake up Grimball, what are you waiting for? Bring me McDuffus!" she repeated loudly.

"Yes Sir. I mean Madam" he saluted.

He was very glad to get away from her icy stare and stance, even for the briefest moment. But he was also afraid for 'Mac', a nickname he had given his old friend of long ago, in better times.

McDuffus was brought before the Queen, yet under questioning he could not remember anything about the day, or even Pipsqueak. It was obvious to Matilda that he had been magically spellbound, which she did not have the power to break. She was bitter that he had betrayed her, so he was arrested, along with Jack, Penelope and Libby.

It was no good, she thought, she would have to lead Grimball and his army herself, and the most likely choice of direction the escapees would have gone, would be towards 'Whispering Woods.'

This was the shortest route to the Crystal Kingdom, and possibly the safest, but she had some of her closest allies amongst the trees, and secrets were never safe in 'Whispering Woods', hence the name. It was just a case of talking to the right contacts to help her discover the whereabouts of the children, which would ultimately lead to their captivity. Then it would be game over for her sister!

****

Charlie was on the outskirts of Whispering Woods in deep thought. He also knew the risks involved in taking this route, but he hoped with strategy, speed and silence, this operation would prove a success and the children would safely arrive at their destination. The alternative road was towards 'Mystical Mountain', but this would take longer, and it was fraught with danger and evil magic. It would take more than wit for safe passage, and so they journeyed on through Whispering Woods.

As the sun began to set and the wind whipped up, Mia and Oakley awoke feeling rather cold and hungry. When they looked around them, they were surprised to see they were surrounded by trees, ranging from big and tall to bushy, short, fat and sturdy. Beneath Lightning's hooves lay a carpet of red, brown and gold leaves, which rustled quietly as she trotted along. Mia couldn't understand how in only a short space of time, summer had turned to autumn! She was about to question this, when Charlie quickly turned to her, and raised the tip of his wing to his beak, signaling silence.

"Where are we?" asked Oakley, ignoring Charlie.

"Ssh!" whispered the cockatoo. The alarm in his voice instantly quietened the children.

He then produced a note from under his wing, which read in bold letters…

'BEWARE OF WHISPERING WOODS. PLEASE REMAIN SILENT AND OUT OF SIGHT UNTIL ALL DANGER IS GONE!'

The children immediately obeyed and nuzzled back down into the comfort and safety of Lightning's mane. However, they were both so very hungry and it wasn't long before their stomachs started rumbling and gurgling, which shattered the silence in the woods.

Unexpectedly there was the biggest rumble of all, and both Mia and Oakley jumped up in fright, looking at each other.

"Stay down!" Charlie commanded from above their heads.

"What is happening Mia? It sounds like a giant with bad wind" jested Oakley but feeling very scared indeed.

"Be quiet Oakley! I'm sure Charlie has everything under control." Had they looked out of their hideaway, they would have seen that they were surrounded by the ugliest 'talking' trees.

"What are you doing in *our* woods?" demanded Lofty, the tallest and most ugly tree in the group.

"And where are you going to?" barked Stump.

"How many in the party?" shouted Twig.

It was like 'Passport Control', but Charlie knew only too well that they could be walking into a trap, as this region was divided in its loyalties.

"I am Charlie the Cockatoo, Royal Messenger of Queen Cristina. And by order I have in my party, Lightning, most beloved unicorn of her majesty, who was stolen by Pixie Pipsqueak. He has been arrested to face justice at the Crystal Court." he lied.

He felt this story was the most believable and hoped they would let Pipsqueak go. He knew he would have to entrust Pipsqueak with the children's safety, but pixies were fast runners and always had plenty of tricks up their sleeves. He

did not fear for Lightning and himself, because they would escape later, but it was important for the children to get away now, before Matilda caught up with them again.

"Where are the children?" Lofty interrupted Charlie's thoughts.

"Oh, the children! But of course, they were hungry! You must have heard their bellies rumbling, so I sent them to go and pick some berries from over there" he pointed out, breathing a sigh of relief for his quick thinking!

"You, Pixie! If it is true, what this cocky cockatoo has to say, go and get the children and bring them back here at once" threatened Lofty.

"No problem!" replied Pipsqueak, pretending he wanted to help. "I'm so grateful to you for my freedom, it's the least I can do!" he added convincingly.

As Pipsqueak went to carry out his orders, Charlie gave him a sly wink, and suddenly flapped and squawked into the sky above, causing Lofty and his friends to stare up in alarm. In the distraction, the little pixie quickly withdrew magical fairy dust from a secret pouch in his jacket, and sprinkled it over the children, who were still hiding in Lightning's mane. In a split second, Mia and Oakley shrunk to the size of two little peas. With delicacy, Pipsqueak picked them up and placed them in his pocket and ran through the woods as fast as he could, far away from danger.

Meanwhile, Charlie had landed back on Lightning, and was full of apologies to Lofty.

"I am *terribly* sorry Sir, about my little outburst, but I felt very insulted when you called me a cockatoo, because I am in fact a *parrot*, and perfect at that!"

"But you said you were Charlie the cockatoo, not Charlie the parrot…" Lofty reminded him.

"Well….cockatoo sounds more regal and parrot is more common" explained Charlie.

Lofty was perplexed, but nevertheless found this strange bird's antics highly amusing. He began to laugh hysterically, his twig-like branches waving to and fro in the air. The next minute all the other trees had joined in, and Pipsqueak and the children had been forgotten.

Charlie continued to entertain the tree folk, telling stories, jokes and somersaulting through the air. He put on such a show that, as Lightning silently trotted away, even her disappearance from the clearing went unnoticed.

The cunning cockatoo knew it was now time to make his exit, and as he flew higher and higher into the air, he noticed Willow, a most beautiful and elegant tree in the distance and an old faithful friend. With one last swoop, down upon Lofty and his mates, he gave a victory roll as he headed towards Willow and safety. He just hoped and prayed it wouldn't be too long before everyone was re-united and the journey to the Crystal Kingdom completed.

8. HOLLY AND IVY

Pipsqueak darted back and forth through the trees, as swiftly and silently as he could, his small dark brown eyes scanning the path ahead. He knew of only one option where the children would be assured safety until they could all meet up again.

It was a glade, inhabited by two beautiful woodland nymphs, 'Holly and Ivy.' They were twin sisters and loyal subjects of Queen Cristina whom would protect the children. Ivy would be their shield, allowing time for rest, whilst Holly would defend them with her thorny branches. She would also be able to provide rich ripe berries, full of goodness, for them to eat.

Mia and Oakley bounced up and down like two rubber balls as Pipsqueak ran along.

"Oh Mia, I feel sick," complained Oakley, his words jumping out of his mouth.

"So, do I," agreed Mia. "But hopefully the danger will soon pass, and we can get back to normality!"

"Does that mean growing up again?" asked Oakley, feeling rather hopeful as he didn't like being the size of a pea, or a mushy pea if Pipsqueak didn't stop running! He started to cry.

"Please stop crying Oakley, or you'll end up like Nanna Jaks 'watery' pea soup!" she joked, hoping to reassure him.

This did the trick for he immediately burst into laughter, remembering the disastrous recipe.

Finally, Pipsqueak stopped running and sighed with relief as he saw the familiar waterfall ahead. Alongside, trailing over the rocks and into the clearing, the sight of Miss Ivy was a blessing in disguise. Although he couldn't see Miss Holly, he knew she couldn't be far, for they were practically inseparable.

Out of the two sisters, Ivy was the nicest, although not the prettiest. She had a kind nature, but being a very 'clingy' vine, Pipsqueak knew he had to be careful, as she loved to cuddle everyone! Mrs. Pipsqueak would certainly not appreciate that sort of behaviour, if she heard it through the 'grapevine!'

Miss Holly was different altogether, very beautiful but a prickly character. You didn't want to get on her 'thorny' side.

However, time was of the essence and he had to do his job, for Queen and country. With a whispered apology to an *invisible* Mrs. Pipsqueak, he sprinted the last few yards, leapt into the air, and nose-dived into the blanket of thick ivy on the ground. Coming to an abrupt halt, the children bounced out of his pocket. As they hit the ground, they immediately returned to their normal size. All three of them sat bolt upright, surveying their surroundings. Everyone began to laugh, relieved that the danger had passed.

Suddenly, a green and willowy nymph arose out of the ivy around them, ignoring Mia and Oakley completely, but directing her attention to Pipsqueak.

"Well! Well! Well! Pipsqueak, that was quite an entrance," she blushed, rushing forward and putting her leafy tendrils around him tightly.

"Did you miss me that much?" she teased.

"Hold on Ivy! There's a time and a place, and we have children present," he reprimanded, trying to break free from her embrace.

"Children…children! How wonderful!" she exclaimed. Upon seeing them, she rushed forward with outstretched arms.

"Be careful Ivy! You'll frighten them, and don't squeeze too hard or you'll squash them," cautioned Pipsqueak, his voice rising with concern.

Mia and Oakley were far from being scared because the nymph reminded them of Nanna Jaks and home! With familiarity, they snuggled closer to her, feeling warm and safe again. It wasn't too long before they were fast asleep, dreaming of the 'Fairy Room' they had long left behind.

****

After a while, Pipsqueak beckoned Ivy to come and speak with him privately. She gently unwrapped herself from the children and glided over to the endearing little pixie, who now seemed so serious. As they spoke in whispers, they didn't notice the children wake up.

Not wanting to interrupt Pipsqueak and Ivy, who were in deep conversation, Mia and Oakley decided to go and explore.

Noticing some beautiful red berries on a 'holly' bush nearby, Oakley was the first to run to it, pick the fruit and pop it in his mouth. Mia was about to do the same when directly, from behind the bush, a most beautiful woodland nymph appeared, but unlike Ivy, she didn't seem as friendly. She gave them a prickly stare which froze them to the spot.

"How dare you children! "Taking the berries from my tree is a serious crime, and you young man will pay the price," she shouted angrily at Oakley, who started to cry for the second time that day. Mia bravely stepped forward to defend her brother.

"Don't be so nasty to my brother," she warned boldly. "We are very hungry and have had such a bad day! We've been turned into peas, chased by trees, and lost our friends," she added defensively.

Suddenly, her little brother collapsed on the grass at her feet. At that moment, Pipsqueak and Ivy hastily hurried over, having heard Mia shouting in the distance.

"Oh dear! Dear! Dear!" cried Ivy. "What've you done Holly?"

"Done…? Done! My dearest sister, you know as well as I do, my berries are not to be picked without my permission, and definitely not to be eaten without mistletoe milk, otherwise they can be most potent!"

"Potent! Doesn't that mean poisonous?" asked Mia anxiously, throwing herself down on the ground and beginning to cry. She grabbed hold of her little brother so tightly to her chest it hurt, but she drew comfort when she could hear his heart beating gently beneath her fingertips.

"Now, sweetheart, don't worry! Everything is going to be alright," soothed Ivy. She looked at her sister for confirmation and support.

"Yes of course! Please stop crying, your brother is only sleeping; he will be fine once he has a sip of mistletoe milk," said Holly, more kindly.

"Then, *please* give him some, to make him better," pleaded Mia.

"I'm so sorry, I'm afraid…" she hesitated, not knowing what to say to allay this young girl's fears completely.

"Oh No! Please don't tell us, you don't have any?!" guessed Pipsqueak, burying his head in his hands.

Ivy rushed to her dear friend, showing her concern, and explained they had been waiting for Mistletoe to arrive with supplies.

Mistletoe was a beautiful nymph, with a reputation for being elusive and difficult to find… She would only visit when it was safe to do so, as Queen Matilda wanted her captivity and the magic milk. It was more than likely she had heard of Matilda's presence in the area, and so had returned to the lake bearing her name, just on the outskirts of Mystical Mountain.

There was a moment of silence in the glade. Pipsqueak knew he had to make a quick decision.

"I will have to seek out Mistletoe alone," he told Holly and Ivy, who acknowledged this was the best option under the circumstances.

"We promise we will keep the children safe, while you're gone," said Ivy reassuringly.

"With my strong fortress of thorns, and my sister's cloak of ivy, no harm will come to the children, you have my word" promised Holly.

Pipsqueak thanked them both. As it was nearly nightfall, he thought it best to wait until morning before setting off in search of this mysterious nymph. He just hoped and prayed that Holly and Ivy would be able to outwit Queen Matilda and safeguard the children until his return.

9. LIGHTNING'S SECRET

The darkness of the night shrouded the land. Pipsqueak was restless and worried about the few days ahead. His mind pondered on what had happened to Charlie and Lightning; he hoped they had escaped and were heading towards Holly and Ivy's Glen, but he couldn't be sure. Matilda would certainly be on the warpath, doing everything in her power to find the children, so it was dangerous for them to stay in one place for too long. Moving Oakley was not an easy task. Pipsqueak knew Mia would not leave without her brother, therefore the best course of action was to find Mistletoe, get some *magic* milk and bring it back as quickly as possible. He could trust Holly and Ivy implicitly to protect the children until his return.

Suddenly, his thoughts were shattered by the sound of hoofbeats in the distance. He held his breath for a second, fearing Matilda and her army were nearby. He knew there was no time to escape, and his heart started racing. What was he going to do? He shut his eyes contemplating his next move, but as he opened them, there in the shadow of the moonlight, he saw Lightning, beautiful as ever, with her glossy white mane and fluorescent alicorn heading towards them.

Pipsqueak rushed forward to greet his friend, feeling immense relief. He told her everything that had happened since they'd parted, then Lightning relayed the story of how Charlie and herself had got away.

"But where is Charlie?" asked Pipsqueak uneasily, looking around for the quirky bird.

"Now don't worry Pipsqueak. The last time I saw Charlie, he was flying towards Willow, a wise old tree and a very good friend of his," reassured Lightning. "But he will not be safe for long, so we must go and get him."

"Get him?!" shrieked Pipsqueak in alarm. "We can't go running back through Whispering Woods again! It's far too dangerous!"

"Who said we're running?" teased Lightning.

"If you're talking magic, I have none left," said Pipsqueak dejectedly.

Lightning laughed heartily.

"Who needs magic when there's a storm brewing?" she replied, with a twinkle in her eye.

Pipsqueak hadn't noticed whilst talking to Lightning, that the wind had indeed whipped up. The sky was growing darker, the clouds were threatening, and a few spots of rain had started to fall. The pair made their way back to the children.

Mia awoke and was greatly surprised to see Lightning. She rushed over to her. The sudden coldness of her skin made Mia shiver, but she didn't care as she was so happy to see her dear friend again.

"There has been a change of plan," informed Pipsqueak. Ivy

and Holly came to listen, leaving Oakley sleeping peacefully on a grassy knoll, oblivious to everything.

"We are leaving straightaway, and we will be taking both children with us," announced Lightning. "It is far too dangerous to leave them with you and endanger yourselves. My intention is to pick up Charlie first, and then continue to Lake Mistletoe, to get the magical milk Oakley needs to awaken him."

Holly and Ivy would have loved for the children to stay longer, as they had become rather fond of them in such a short space of time, but they agreed the unicorn's plan was safer.

"Can you help me?" said Lightning, her big blue eyes gazing down on Mia hypnotically.

"Of course!" replied Mia, without any hesitation.

Lightning turned around and walked to a nearby clearing, shouting instructions to everyone, as they proceeded to follow her.

"Bring the boy Ivy!"

"Fetch the crystal Mia!"

"Stay close Pipsqueak!"

"Watch for intruders Holly!"

They all obeyed in silence, as Lightning took her place in the middle of the clearing and started to kick up the dust beneath her feet. She then ordered Pipsqueak to start running as fast as he could around her in circles, creating more dust. They were both barely visible and the sound of distant thunder was getting closer. From within the circle, Mia heard Lightning's voice reach out to her.

"Throw the crystal into the centre of the dust-cloud… now!" shouted Lightning.

Mia hurled the stone into the air, and as it touched down with accurate precision, there was an explosion of popping light bulbs so dazzling, she had to shield her eyes.

"Oh No! Bluebell's crystal has shattered… I have destroyed her home!" Mia cried out in anguish.

Ivy rushed forward to comfort and cocoon her, as she stood with her head in her hands ready to cry.

"Look up my dear, everything is fine" she consoled her.

Mia gazed up and couldn't believe her eyes. There in front of her, stood Lightning with the most beautiful pair of wings fluttering in the stormy breeze. Raindrops glistened on her white silky feathers like stardust.

"Wow!" she exclaimed, sounding like her brother.

"Ready to go Mia," smiled Lightning.

She nodded her head approvingly, not really knowing what had just happened. Ivy then explained that by using the crystal, she had summoned the Lightning fairy to work her magic.

"I still don't fully understand," said Mia.

"Well let me explain!" continued Holly. "Lightning is no ordinary unicorn. With a storm and a little bit of magic, this special fairy has the power to give her wings to fly, either night or day, out of any dangerous situation."

"I see," she replied, a little mesmerised by it all.

"Don't forget the crystal," interrupted Lightning, which Mia saw lying brightly on the ground near her silken hooves. She ran over to pick it up and was glad to see it had not been damaged. Without any further ado, she placed it safely back in her pocket.

Finally, it was time to say goodbye and leave the glen behind. Holly was the first to step forward and present Mia with two swords made from her thorny branches, each wrapped in a thick grassy sheath.

"These will protect you and Oakley from any dangers you may encounter," she advised. Then, seeing the sudden apprehension on the little girl's face, she concluded. "I am sure everything is going to be alright child!"

"And I have made you two coats of ivy, to wear when the weather gets colder," added Ivy, feeling rather tearful now they were departing.

"Thank you so much," said Mia gratefully. "Hopefully my brother and I will see you again sometime."

She smiled at them both as she went to climb upon Lightning. Pipsqueak placed Oakley in front of her, and she held on to him very tightly, feeling his breath against her cheek. She longed for him to be his normal talkative self and hoped they would find Charlie and Mistletoe soon.

"Right everybody! Hold on tight! It's time for take-off!" directed Lightning.

"Did somebody say *Time?*!" came a familiar voice from behind a nearby rock.

"Oh…it's you Tick Tock!" laughed Mia. "What are you doing here?"

"Well…I've been watching you all and thought you might need some more time!"

"Time for what?" asked Mia, feeling very confused.

"Time to eat…time to play…time to say goodbye…or time to get away!" joked Tick Tock.

Mia found this delightful little elf so funny and cute, with his clockwork eyes, which she hadn't noticed before. As usual, he was wearing a giant hour glass necklace and holding his watch like wand. She was grateful for his help, and knew they did in fact, need more time to get Charlie. As soon as the storm abated, it wouldn't be long before Lightning's wings disappeared, and she became her normal self again.

Mia didn't hesitate, she knew it was the best thing to do. Turning to Tick Tock, she said, "My dearest friend Tick Tock, please turn back time!"

On Mia's instruction, Tick Tock turned the hourglass upside down and the sands of time slowly passed backwards to the very beginning of the storm. As Lightning flew high into the dark sky, with her passengers safely on board, they all waved a final farewell to Holly and Ivy, in the woodland below.

10. 'BAT ATTACK'

Queen Matilda had arrived in Whispering Woods. She was furious that Lofty and his band of tree fellows had also allowed the children to escape so easily. Grimball was glad her temper was now directed on somebody else.

"You idiot!" she ranted at Lofty. "I've a good mind to chop you down and use you for firewood. You call yourself my special branch...hah!"

"Please forgive me Ma'am, it was that clever cockatoo Charlie! He hoodwinked us all with his lies and fancy acrobatic tricks; we didn't even notice the children get away," whimpered Lofty.

"Enough of your feeble excuses! You are all fools!" she bellowed, looking at Twig and Stumpy, with anger and contempt for them too.

Stumpy, who was the boldest of the three, stepped forward.

"Excuse me your highness, but I think I know where Charlie is," he said hesitantly, thinking this revelation would calm Matilda down, but unfortunately it did not.

"Charlie! I am not interested in Charlie! It is the children I want. They are my biggest threat and need to be stopped," she screamed, her face turning as red as beetroot. Stumpy stood frozen to the spot not daring to speak another word or move.

"Everything's fine, everything's okay, nothing to worry about!" interrupted Twig, being the most diplomatic of the three. He prattled on, hardly taking a breath, in case Matilda silenced him with her evil stare and venomous mouth. He must act the hero and save them all from being turned into kindle.

"Stumpy is right Ma'am! Charlie is now with Willow, his tree pal for many years, and is waiting for the rest of the party to join him."

Matilda was about to question this, but for once she decided to keep quiet, and let Twig continue.

"There is no doubt about this rendezvous, as Charlie is the only one who can escort the children safely through Mystical Mountain and into the Crystal Kingdom," confirmed Twig

"But why would he take the children through such treacherous territory?" queried Matilda.

"Because we've found out that the boy has eaten 'slumber berries' and needs Mistletoe milk to awaken him" butted in Stumpy, regaining his confidence.

Suddenly Matilda's demeanour totally changed, and she smiled for once, showing just how beautiful she really was!

"Job well done my dear friends!" she said smugly. "We now have to decide the best plan of action to take to capture these children, which will settle this matter once and for all! At last, I feel we have the upper hand," she sniggered.

"I have a plan," said Lofty meekly, now coming forward out of the shadows where he had been hiding in shame from the Queen. "We will surround Willow and wait in silence for the others to join Charlie, and then we will ambush!"

"Ambush! Ambush!" cackled Matilda. Lofty was not sure whether the queen thought this was a good idea or not, but when his friends started tittering too, he felt a little relieved.

"Why… that's a tree-mendous idea, as long as we don't go barking up the wrong tree," she ridiculed them. She began to laugh hysterically at her own joke, even though Lofty, Twig and Stumpy were far from amused.

Lofty was about to speak up, when her manner becoming more serious, she continued "Enough of this tree-foolery! Grimball, get ready to march your army towards the vicinity of Willow and Charlie immediately."

"Lofty, Twig and Stumpy, alert all branches in the area to watch for any signs of movement on the ground, or in the sky," she commanded abruptly, still angry with them for letting the children escape in the first place.

****

Meanwhile, Charlie was unaware of Matilda's plans and was most concerned for the safety of the children, and his friends. He was conveying his anxiety to Willow, who listened patiently.

"Don't worry my old friend," she consoled. "I am sure

Lightning will find Pipsqueak and the children, and you will all be reunited soon."

"Oh Willow, I do hope you are right, but I'm afraid it will not be safe for me to stay here too long because if Matilda finds me, we are both going to be in *hubble bubble*."

Willow was also apprehensive, as she knew Matilda would be searching for him just as much as the children. He was important to the mission, and without him to guide the way, Mia and Oakley would not reach the safety of the Crystal Kingdom. With her spies everywhere, Matilda would easily discover his whereabouts and thwart any further plans he had. To distract her dear friend, she started to talk about better times.

Unexpectedly, it started to rain, very gently at first, followed by a rumble of thunder in the distance. Charlie took shelter in a small nook in Willow's bark, as the rain became torrential. He was not sure whether this was a good or bad sign at first, but the sudden bolt of lightning shooting through the sky overhead indicated help was on the way.

Just as the rain began, Matilda was approaching. She could see clearly ahead the location of Willow and Charlie and was ecstatic to think there was no way out for this troublesome cockatoo. With her was a small party of gnomes, and a battalion of bats at her call.

"Charlie are you awake?" whispered Willow.

"Sure am matey! I can see trouble on the ground, but I can

also see hope in the heavens above!" said Charlie enthusiastically.

"I don't think it's going to be easy," warned Willow.

"Nothing ever is," replied Charlie, but he trusted Lightning to rescue him from the clutches of Matilda, who was swiftly advancing towards them.

Willow proceeded to watch their enemies getting closer, whilst Charlie searched for Lightning, in the murky skies overhead.

"Where is she?" he thought out aloud, growing more concerned and impatient.

Willow directed her gaze upwards now, feeling just as anxious and worried as Charlie. She prayed that the unicorn would appear soon, before it was too late.

In a flash, there she was in all her fine glory and splendour, her alicorn shining intensely, illuminating the dark sky. As she circled above, they could see nearby, a gloomy shadow of bats ascending towards her. It was time for immediate action.

"I'm so sorry I have to leave you this way Willow!" said Charlie, with sadness in his voice.

"It's okay Charlie! I'll be fine. Go... quickly now... I'll do all I can to hold the little critters back," she assured him.

"Thanks Willow!" Charlie saluted her, and without further hesitation, flew high up into the midnight sky, heading directly towards Lightning. As the bats approached, Willow began to

wave her branches vigorously back and forth in defence, knocking some of the ugly creatures senseless and sending them to the ground.

Through the dark clouds below, Lightning could see some of the bats had escaped Willow's attack and were now quickly flying towards them. For a brief second, she felt alarmed, but then to her delight, saw her familiar colourful friend soaring through the atmosphere.

"Wake up Mia," prompted Lightning. On hearing the unicorn's startled voice, Mia woke up immediately.

"What's wrong?" she shouted, not happy at being disturbed from her slumber.

"Remove the swords of holly from their sheaths! "You keep one and give the other to Pipsqueak," ordered Lightning. "We are *under attack*, and it's now time for you to be brave!"

"*Under attack*!" shrieked Mia, as she withdrew the swords from the depths of Lightning's mane and handed one to Pipsqueak, whose hand was already outstretched in readiness.

"Bats Mia!" confirmed Pipsqueak. "We have to fight them off until Charlie is on board."

"Charlie!" exclaimed Mia excitedly, forgetting her fear for a minute. She looked around her and downward into the night sky, when she saw the cheeky cockatoo making his way towards them, followed by a ghoulish black cloud. She now realised the seriousness of the situation. As she searched for the crystal deep in her pocket and wondered if there was any magic she could conjure up to help, she suddenly felt unusually calm and courageous. Holding the sword of holly firmly in her hand, she raised it high in the air, ready for battle.

The bats were now in front of Charlie, ignoring him as they passed by, and instead flying directly to their target. Matilda had ordered them to surround the unicorn and her precious party and force them to the ground. However, they hadn't reckoned on the expertise of Mia and Pipsqueak, as they wielded their leafy weapons. Even the glare of Lightning's alicorn blinded them from getting too near. Finally, they decided to retreat, and as they flew away to face the wrath of Queen Matilda, Charlie landed safely on Lightning, taking his position on top of the alicorn.

"Cor blimey! Am I glad to see you, me mateys!" he squawked, feeling a little breathless. "That sure was some 'batty' battle," he joked, making light of all that had just happened.

"Oh Charlie!" cried Mia. "I am so glad you're alright. We have all missed you so much!"

Lightning and Pipsqueak smiled at their cockney friend with joy and relief.

"Well now everybody's here, it's time we headed for Lake Mistletoe," announced Lightning.

"Yes of course! Lead the way, my good ol' chum!" replied Charlie, becoming more serious.

The storm was beginning to abate, and the dawn was breaking. Before long Lightning would return to her normal *wingless* self, and time would resume once more, so they needed to get as near to the lake as possible, before the magic was gone.

11. AUTUMN VALLEY

Mia fell asleep soundly on Lightning's back, buried beneath her soft warm mane, her arms wrapped tightly around Oakley. The night's adventure had tired her out, but she felt very proud of herself for the courage she had shown. She was also happy to have Charlie back.

When she awoke, she noticed they were all safely back on the ground in a beautiful forest of autumnal trees. Although the sun was shining, there was a coolness in the breeze.

"Hello there sleepyhead!" teased Charlie, making her jump in surprise.

"Oh, good morning Charlie! Where are we?" she asked.

"Autumn Valley! I was hoping we would make it further along to Winter Valley, but that's magic for you..." said Charlie disappointedly.

"Oh dear! Does that mean our journey is going to take longer, which could mean more danger?" she replied, her concern growing for all of them again.

"Not necessarily, for I have decided to send Pipsqueak ahead to find Mistletoe, and then meet us at Snowball's hideaway," reassured Charlie.

"It will save time Mia, if we all meet up at Snowball's!" added Lightning.

"I understand, but who is Snowball?" questioned Mia.

"Snowball is a snowman of course!" answered Charlie sarcastically.

"Captain Snowball actually, who has won many campaigns in his lifetime and has the medals to prove it," he explained, in honour of his icy friend.

Mia couldn't wait to meet the infamous Snowball and mysterious Mistletoe! This adventure was proving to be so exciting; she felt sorry for her brother who was missing it all, but she would delight in telling him the story so far when he awoke.

"Are you hungry Mia?" Charlie interrupted her thoughts, hearing her stomach grumble loudly.

"Well it sounds like it! I had completely forgotten about food, but now you mention it, shall I go and search for some berries, or a lake to fish in?"

"I don't think so Mia. It would be safer to stay away from berries and fish after previous incidents…" joked Charlie.

Mia laughed, her stomach grumbling even louder.

"I suggest you summon the *food fairy*," mocked Lightning.

"Food Fairy!" exclaimed Mia, looking at Lightning with curiosity. She noticed how tired the unicorn seemed. Charlie had noticed too, and realised his friend still needed time to rest and recover from the previous night's ordeal. But they had to keep moving. It was not safe for the children to stay in one place for too long with Matilda hot on their heels, so he had to decide the best plan of action for everyone.

Mia was thinking about the *Food Fairy* whilst subconsciously rubbing the crystal deep inside her pocket, when suddenly, she became aware of the silence around her. As she looked up, she saw a beautiful red, orange and yellow orb glowing in the trees and moving towards them. She stood still in awe. Charlie and Lightning knew who this magical visitor was, and so waited patiently for her to transform.

"Princess Autumn!" said Charlie humbly, bowing as low as he could before her in admiration. Lightning bowed her head too, and with etiquette, Mia gracefully curtseyed. She was the most stunning fairy Mia had ever seen, with glittering wings of autumn coloured leaves, green iridescent eyes and long auburn curls.

"I apologise for Miss Mia, if she accidentally summoned you… I'm afraid she is a *newbie* to the power of crystals," he explained, looking at Mia with suspicion.

Mia was about to protest, when Autumn interrupted and spoke with a gentle and soothing melodic voice.

"The girl did not summon me Charlie. I was informed by Bluebell to keep a look-out for the protector of her crystal, so I have been drawn to you to offer my help in any way I can."

Mia stepped forward, eager to meet this beautiful fairy.

"Are you the 'Food Fairy?" she asked, her stomach groaning yet again!

"I am not!" laughed Autumn, "but I can hear that you're rather hungry, so if you would like to look in that picnic basket over there, you may find something delicious to eat."

She pointed to a group of trees nearby whose branches were practically bare. Their discarded leaves looked like a rustic carpet on the ground; perched on top of the pile was a small hamper. Mia was very grateful and immediately ran over to investigate the contents.

"Thank you so much!" she said politely, delving deep into the basket.

Charlie chuckled as he watched the little girl eat a cheeseburger, followed by fries and a milkshake. He knew whatever she wished for would magically appear. It was just a shame Oakley was missing out. It worried him even more to think the boy was still far from getting the cure he needed to awaken him. Hopefully, Autumn would be able to assist them in some way.

Reading Charlie's thoughts, Autumn glided nearer to him and outlined her plan.

"Don't worry Charlie! All will be well. Lightning can remain here and rest under my protection until she is able to join you… But I understand the necessity to get the children to Winter Valley as soon as possible. My magic will take you there," she reassured him.

Charlie trusted Autumn completely. With a sense of relief, he joined Mia to indulge in *his favourite* appetisers. When full, he pulled out lots of apples and sweet mown hay for Lightning and carried them over to her.

"Hey Lightning girl! Eat this! It will rebuild your strength," he advised.

"Thank you, Charlie!" she gratefully replied.

"I have been speaking to Autumn and we both think you should stay here until you have fully recovered. You can then meet us in Winter Valley, at Snowball's hideaway," instructed Charlie.

Lightning sighed deeply, feeling more relaxed, and after eating as much as she could, she laid down on the ground and fell fast asleep.

****

Autumn and Mia were fast becoming friends. They chased each other around the glen, played hide n' seek, and then had a leaf fight. The game ended abruptly when Mia was so covered in leaves, she didn't resemble a little girl anymore. As she ran around looking like a leafy shrub and shrieking loudly, everyone burst into raucous laughter.

However, the time for fun had come to an end; the journey had to continue.

"Well Mia! I've had a ball, but I'm afraid it's time for you, your brother and Charlie to leave," said Autumn sadly.

"I want you and Charlie to gather as many twigs, leaves, moss and lichen as you can and place them in a pile. I have already collected sap from the trees," she told them.

"Are we making some sort of nest?" enquired Mia, brushing herself down in readiness to help this beautiful fairy. She remembered watching a nature programme about this back home.

Autumn thought how intuitive this little girl was for one so young and smiled encouragingly.

Charlie and Mia collected the necessary items until Autumn told them to stop. She then added the milky white *magical* sap. As it flowed through every fibre, the nest became bigger, more solid and secure. To Mia's astonishment, it was now a suitable vehicle to transport them to safety.

"Are you ready to go Mia?" she asked.

Mia nodded her head positively. She gathered her brother into her arms and stepped aboard. She didn't know what to expect, but observing there were no wheels present, she was beginning to feel rather excited.

"Charlie take the lead," directed Autumn.

"Certainly, your highness," he replied proudly.

Autumn rose high above them, spinning and twirling. She created such a breeze, it lifted the nest above the ground. It hovered slowly at first and then gathering momentum, it started to move speedily through the glen. Fallen leaves were swept up and thrown out of its pathway. It reminded Mia of a 'rollercoaster' ride; it was so fast and exhilarating! She wasn't scared as she could see Charlie ahead, directing the vehicle so they didn't crash into anything. To her amazement, she also noticed they were being flanked by a group of tree elves whose leafy wings shielded the vehicle from being seen. Autumn had thought of everything.

Holding Oakley tightly, she looked behind to see that Autumn had vanished out of sight, along with Lightning.

"Thank you, dear Autumn! May we meet again someday," she whispered on the breeze, as they journeyed towards Winter Valley.

12. MATILDA'S PLAN

As Charlie steered the *nest* car safely through the autumn glen whilst the tree elves continued to protect the children from discovery, Queen Matilda was thinking about her next move. She was so annoyed that her 'bat' attack hadn't succeeded, and even more upset to learn of the Autumn Fairy's intervention, which she hadn't counted on. This was yet another drawback, and she hated to admit it, but they were winning! She must stop them from reaching the Crystal Kingdom, or she would lose her realm.

"Grimball! Come here!" she ordered, pointing her finger at the fat grizzly gnome, sitting quietly by the campfire with his men. He jumped up promptly on her summons and ran over to her.

"Yes… your majesty?" he stammered.

"Tell me Grimball…What would *you* do in my position?" she asked.

"Do Ma'am? Well if it were me I'd…" feeling a little confused by her question, since she never asked for anyone's help or opinion, he began to babble. It was so odd to see her lacking in self- confidence. Her apparent deflation made him almost feel sorry for her.

"Stop dithering and answer me Grimball!" she bellowed.

"Sorry Ma'am," he apologised, looking at the ground in embarrassment. He began to twitch and mutter to himself, an annoying habit of his, when he was either nervous or stuck for words. Gaining his composure, he thought for just a brief second before he proceeded with diplomatic decorum.

"My advice is not to give up the chase, but to be *positive*, be *brave* and be *smart*!"

"Well said Grimball, but I don't want to hear a lot of fancy words," she replied sarcastically. "I need to know what action to take to achieve *success*, *victory* and *ultimate power*," she added, mocking him.

Grimball realised that he had to choose his next words very carefully; not only was his reputation at stake, but he could also lose his position as head of the army. It was imperative that he gave Matilda the answer she was looking for... "I think we should capture Mistletoe," he suggested after some serious thought.

"Capture Mistletoe?" shrieked Matilda. "What good will that do us?" She thought Grimball had lost his senses and her disappointment in him was growing. She felt inclined to dismiss him there and then.

"Hear me out, your majesty," continued Grimball. "We know they are still looking for Mistletoe, as they need her magic milk to awaken the boy from his deep slumber. They must obtain this, before they proceed with their journey. Without it, the quest will be thwarted and the battle over, for the girl cannot win on her own."

"Brilliant Grimball!" enthused Matilda, her face lighting up with an evil grin.

"We will head towards Lake Mistletoe and I will notify Frost and Friends to be at the ready. *This* time we will *not* be beaten," she cackled.

"Get your men ready! There is no time to waste, we are leaving *immediately*," she commanded.

Grimball went to protest, as he knew his men would not be too happy with these orders. Nightfall was imminent, and they needed to rest, but one scornful look from his queen silenced him. As he made his way back to the campsite, he crossed his fingers firmly behind his back and whispered into the night air "Third time lucky, please!"

****

The dawn was breaking when they finally reached the outskirts of Lake Mistletoe, and Grimball's army were tired and fretful. Matilda had made it very clear that they were not going to stop until the woodland nymph had been found and captured. Grimball knew she could be anywhere on this vast lake, but he was hoping she had returned to the safety of the copse nearby, where mistletoe shrubs grew in abundance. He was surveying the lake when suddenly he saw her, as beautiful as ever. Her tall willowy body and delicate features glowed in the sunlight, as she strolled along the shore gently kicking up the water beneath her feet. Her long silvery white tresses floated behind her on the autumnal breeze and he was mesmerized.

"Colonel Grimball! There she is sir! What do we do next?" asked Schmitz, a young and eager soldier looking to advance his position in the ranks.

Grimball was instantly awakened from his reverie.

"Advance men but keep your heads down and bodies close to the ground. We do not want to scare her away," he commanded.

As planned, Matilda was waiting with a group of gnomes in the copse. She also saw Mistletoe at the water's edge and felt triumphant because she knew the nymph was trapped. Many times, she had ventured to this region to try and capture her but had been outsmarted by Mistletoe's ability to transform into the shrub she protected. It was impossible to tell them apart for the transformation was always carried out discreetly, but this time there would be no escape.

"Bring me the red cape," ordered Matilda.

"Here you are ma'am!" replied Schmell, running forward with the cape outstretched in his arms.

"Quickly, place it over me and then all of you get out of sight and be quiet," she whispered.

As Schmell put the cape on Matilda, she completely disappeared. Everybody stood in awe and wondered how the queen had come by this magical cloak, but no one dared ask. Schmell ordered his comrades to move farther back and take cover.

****

Meanwhile, Pipsqueak had just arrived to see Grimball and his men crawling their way along the ground towards Mistletoe, who was completely oblivious to her fate.

"Run Mistletoe! Run! It's a trap!" he screeched, as he ran as fast as he could towards them.

Mistletoe looked up to see Pipsqueak heading in her direction and waving his arms frantically. She hadn't quite heard what he had said, but it seemed obvious he was trying to warn her. Suddenly, she saw Grimball's army rising only a few yards ahead of her. She had no choice but to get to the copse as quickly as possible. Pipsqueak followed her, managing to avoid Grimball's men, and as soon as they entered the clearing, he saw her transform alongside the other mistletoe shrubs. The chase was over, and he felt she was now safe from captivity. He however, was still being pursued, and so kept running.

"You're not so lucky this time" laughed Matilda, as she cast the invisible cloak to the ground, and walked over to the bush, which Mistletoe had turned into.

"You can stay like that if you wish, but one way or another, you are coming with me," she sneered.

"Men…dig her up!" she ordered smugly.

"What are we going to do with her?" asked Grimball, now joining Matilda. He should have felt victorious, yet he was deeply concerned for the beautiful nymph.

"She can be taken back to the palace to either grow in my garden, or serve me," she screeched.

"And you and I, Grimball, we are going to join Jack Frost and Friends for the final battle!" she shouted triumphantly.

Her voice echoed throughout the glen, and Pipsqueak was near enough to hear every word. He felt not only sad for Mistletoe, but for Mia, who was waiting patiently for the magic milk to awaken her brother. He had failed, but he needed to let his friends know that he had done his best.

89

He had to warn them Matilda was heading their way with her notorious ally Jack Frost, and so it was with a heavy heart that he journeyed on to Captain Snowball's cave.

13. LAKE MISTLETOE

"Halt!" shouted Charlie, as they exited the forest.

"Where are we?" asked Mia, feeling a little disappointed that the magical ride was over.

"It's as far as the elves can take us," replied Charlie, turning to them and acknowledging their help.

"Oh, thank you so much," said Mia gratefully. With a fluttering of wings, they were gone, whisked away on the breeze, leaving the sleigh behind with Oakley still fast asleep inside.

Mia looked around in bewilderment. Stretched out before them was a beautiful grassy plain scattered with daisies and buttercups; but even more captivating was the lake beyond. Blue rippling waves glistened like satin in the sunlight and lapped gently at the bank. On the other side of the water, mountains stood tall and magnificent with their snow-capped peaks barely visible in the misty clouds above.

"Lake Mistletoe!" declared Charlie proudly.

"And Mystical Mountain," stated Mia, in wonder. She knew it was not going to be an easy task for Pipsqueak to locate Mistletoe on this lake, for it stretched for miles.

"Now don't ya worry Miss," reassured Charlie, noticing her concern. "You and I are going to make our way to Captain Snowball's cave and wait there for Pipsqueak, Mistletoe and Lightning. We will be safe there, and once we are all together, we will make our final journey into the Crystal Kingdom."

"But how are we going to get across the lake to Mystical Mountain, and then to Snowball's cave?" she queried. She knew Matilda would be looking for them, so they had to keep moving. If only they had more time to wait for Lightning, but even Tick Tock was nowhere to be seen. Feeling the situation was hopeless, she threw herself down on the grass despondently and began to cry.

"Don't give up hope Mia! You must keep on believing!" comforted Charlie.

Deep in thought, she began to idly pick the buttercups and daisies from the soft verdant grass, her fingers working nimbly and effortlessly until she had made a long lengthy chain.

"Well I never Mia! That sure is the longest daisy 'rope' chain I've ever seen!" interrupted Charlie.

"Rope...? Rope! I've got it!" said Mia excitedly.

"Got it! Got what?" asked Charlie, flapping his wings in confusion.

"We have the 'nest' vehicle, which should float…Right?" she suggested, looking at him for confirmation.

"Sure will, me darlin!" he agreed in his cockney twang.

"Then *you* can use the rope I've made to pull us across the lake! With a bit of belief and magic, we should reach the other side safely," she emphasized.

"Well done gal! What a *clever- clogs* you are! Let's get started," encouraged Charlie, glad to see this pretty little girl's face now glowing with confidence.

Mia withdrew the crystal from her pocket and, touching the daisy chain lightly, she wished it to be as strong as the gemstone she held in her hand. Immediately, it's length and width glowed and strengthened. The petals of the daisies and buttercups became even more beautiful, as every detail was enlarged. It reminded Mia of an Easter garland Nanna Jak's had made for the festival back home.

She tied one end of it to the nest car, which would now act as a boat to get them across the lake, and the other end she gave to Charlie.

"Are you ready Charlie?" she asked, taking charge of the operation and moving the vehicle nearer to the water's edge to launch it, making sure Oakley was securely inside.

"Ready when you are Miss," replied Charlie, thinking how grown up Mia had become in such a short space of time.

He placed the magical garland in his beak and hovered just above the boat, until Mia had jumped in. He proceeded to pull the boat across the lake, flying just high enough to take up the slack of the rope.

As they slowly sailed towards Mystical Mountain, Mia made herself comfortable, cradling her brother beside her. As she relaxed, she thought of everything that had happened since their adventure had begun: the new friends they'd made, and the places they'd passed through. As they neared Mystical Mountain, it seemed to get colder, so Mia reached for the ivy jackets which had been especially made for them. She put Oakley's on him first, then her own, just as they were ready to embark on the shore.

Looking up at the enormous snowy precipice before them, she realised the difficulty they faced reaching the top. Charlie was thinking the same, and he doubted they would make it without magical intervention. Mia was the first to break the silence.

"What are we going to do now Charlie?" she questioned. "It's going to be impossible to use the nest vehicle up the mountain, even with the rope. It'll just be torn apart over the rugged rocks," she admitted.

Charlie remained silent, contemplating what to do next. He was worried about the dilemma they were in and wondered if Lightning was making her way towards them. Although she'd been told to meet them at Captain Snowball's cave, there must be some way to let her know their current situation. This would solve everything, as she was nimble and strong-footed and could carry the children safely up the mountain. Suddenly, he knew what had to be done.

"Mia, where are the stars Twinkle gave you?" he asked.

"I think they're still in Oakley's pocket," she replied.

"Take only one of them out of the bag and be very careful," cautioned Charlie.

Mia did exactly as she was told, and holding the bright star delicately in her hand, she looked at Charlie for further instruction.

"Cast the star into the sky and make a wish that Lightning will see it, and be quickly guided to us," he directed.

Mia hadn't really noticed that the night was drawing in, and as she threw the little star like a boomerang into the dark sky above, it illuminated like a beacon directly overhead. Now all they had to do was wait.

14. MYSTICAL MOUNTAIN

Lightning had fully recovered after resting in the Autumn Forest, and she was most grateful for the protection of the tree elves. She was not far from Lake Mistletoe when she saw Twinkle's star in the sky above, signalling the location of Charlie and the children. She was glad she had regained her strength for it was clear that she was going to need it. Firstly, she would have to swim across the lake to meet her companions, and then climb the rocky mountainside with the children on her back. Lightning knew it would be challenging and treacherous, but once they'd all reached higher ground, the journey would become easier. The night was clear, except for the luminous star guiding Lightning to her friends in need.

It was nearly an hour before Lightning emerged from the lake, her hair wet and glossy. Mia ran to her, hugging her body and kissing her nose, delighted to have her dear friend back.

"I'm glad to see you again!" said Charlie smiling affectionately. "But before we all go any further, you need to rest a while," advised the smart cockatoo.

"I agree," replied Mia, wagging her finger at Lightning, who was about to protest.

"Okay," sighed Lightning. "It seems I'm outnumbered… But as soon as I get my breath back, we're heading up the mountain. You must realise Matilda would have seen the guiding star as well, and is possibly making her way towards us, so it would be stupid to rest for too long."

Charlie and Mia nodded in agreement.

When feeling more refreshed, they decided to ascend Mystical Mountain. Mia took her usual place with her brother in the warm depth of Lightning's mane, and Charlie sat on her alicorn leading the way. The journey seemed endless and the summit so far away, but eventually they reached the top. Although exhausted, the weary travellers were relieved that no accidents or incidences with Matilda had occurred. They hoped Pipsqueak had found Mistletoe without too much trouble and was now making his way to Captain Snowball's cave, where they had all arranged to meet.

Mia was stunned by the beauty of her surroundings. Pure soft snow glistened with the break of dawn like thousands of crystals illuminated by the golden sun. Fresh-scented copses of trees stood majestically against the grey mountains, their summits shrouded by a white frosting.

"This is "Winter Valley," informed Charlie, with pride in his voice.

"Where you will find the 'Mystical Mountain' range," added Lightning.

"Does that mean there is more than one mystical mountain?" questioned Mia.

"That is true Miss, but you needn't worry your little head about that now. We need to get to Snowball's cave at once," replied Charlie.

"Can't we rest again? I'm still feeling tired, *and* quite hungry," complained Mia. It had been a long and arduous journey so far. They'd travelled through the middle of the night, which all agreed was the safest option, but now the remote landscape ahead and rising sun meant the danger was even greater.

"It is far safer to keep moving," warned Charlie, who was already flying ahead and beckoning them on. Mia noticed he kept circling and swooping downwards, as if searching for something, when he unexpectedly nose-dived into a mound of snow, almost burying himself. All she could see was his tail feathers flapping, kicking up the snow in a flurry around him. She quickly jumped off Lightning and ran to his aid.

"Charlie! Are you alright?" she said anxiously, thinking her dear friend had fallen with exhaustion.

"Perhaps we should rest after all," she suggested, but Charlie continued to flap about in the snow, completely ignoring her. She then realised he was looking for something.

"Let me help you," she offered, delving into the snow even though she didn't know what they were looking for. Again, she wished that Oakley was awake to join in. Finally, Charlie emerged from the snow briskly shaking his feathers. Shivering from the coldness of the white powdery substance, he was looking very proud of himself. In his beak he held a small silver whistle, which he began to blow loudly. As he did so, he circled the near vicinity. She began to think her friend had gone 'snow' crazy, but Lightning was quick to reassure her.

"It will be okay Mia. Just wait and see," said Lightning, with a twinkle in her eye. Feeling calmer, she now climbed back onto Lightning's back, where it was warmer. She watched Charlie proceed to fly around them, continuously blowing the silver whistle. Mia hoped Matilda wasn't in earshot to hear it, otherwise another battle could be imminent.

Trembling with this thought uppermost in her mind, she suddenly saw in the distance what seemed like a snowstorm heading towards them.

As she buried herself deeper into Lightning's mane, she waited for the inevitable. Clutching the crystal once again, she asked to be brave, courageous, and to believe that everything would be fine.

Soon the storm was engulfing them, but it felt unusually calm and comforting.

"Open your eyes Mia," said a soothing voice. "You're safe now."

Mia gently opened her eyes, and amid a cascade of snowflakes, hovered a beautiful fairy with white hair and wings.

"Oh…you are so pretty!" declared Mia, in total admiration. She was very relieved not to be facing Matilda.

"Why… thank you! My name is Fairy Snow and I'm here to escort you to Captain Snowball's cave, along with my sister Icicle," she confirmed.

Mia wanted to laugh at the name of Fairy Snow, because it reminded her of Nanna Jaks' washing powder, but she managed to refrain from doing so.

"Where is your sister? I'd like to meet her too," she asked politely, becoming more inquisitive.

"Here I am," said a high-pitched voice. A dainty fairy with sharp features, frosty wings and silver hair that shimmered in the sunlight, came into view from behind Fairy Snow.

"Be careful Icy! Don't come too close or your breath will freeze the child into a human statue, and we don't want that," cautioned Snow.

Mia took a step back, realising that like Holly and Ivy, these two sisters were very different. Although the smallest, Icy was a force to be reckoned with, but Mia felt safe in their company.

Charlie and Lightning came forward to greet the two winter fairies, feeling grateful for their powerful protection, which would lessen the danger of reaching Snowball's cave.

It was decided that Charlie would take the lead, followed by Lightning and the children. Fairy Snow would protect everyone in a cloud of snow, whilst Icicle would cover their tracks on the path behind with frost, so they're footprints could not be followed. If necessary, she could also turn enemies into ice statues if they got too near.

As they travelled onwards, Mia once more buried herself deep into Lightning's mane, holding her brother closely. She prayed that Pipsqueak had found Mistletoe, so it wouldn't be long before Oakley received the magic milk to awaken him, and they could complete their final journey to the Crystal Kingdom.

15. CAPTAIN SNOWBALL'S CAVE

"Wake up Mia!" whispered Fairy Snow. "It's time to meet Captain Snowball."

"Oh, I'm sorry. I must've fallen asleep again," apologised Mia, stretching and yawning, and rubbing her eyes to focus on her new surroundings.

As the mist cleared from her sleepy eyes, she noticed towering monuments of giant snowmen standing regimentally before her in a semi-circle. In their midst was a small cave, barely visible at first glance. The silence was eerie, and Mia wondered where this celebrated captain was, for there were no other animated signs of life, other than their small party.

Without warning, Charlie blew the silver whistle and Mia jumped into the air. She lost her balance and fell from Lightning into the deep marshmallow snow around her. As she raised her head, she saw an army of snowmen, starting with the smallest and escalating in size, emerge from the cave. There were too many to count, and some of them were more like snowballs than snowmen, all with smiley faces. Mia was speechless.

"Captain Snowball at your command!" announced the largest and plumpest snowball of them all, with the cheekiest grin.

Mia couldn't believe her eyes, this was no snowman! He reminded her of an oversized cuddly *emoji* cushion that Oakley had on his bed back home.

"Hello," replied Mia, gaining her composure and standing up to address the Captain, who was no taller than herself. She would never have believed his status, but it was evident in the medals that adorned his *snowy* chest.

He now turned his attention to Charlie and spoke in a more military fashion.

"Royal Commander, I must congratulate you on your mission so far! It has been no easy task, but hopefully together we can achieve a successful result."

"I agree Captain, and as soon as Private Pipsqueak is here, we will be able to continue," advised Charlie.

"Good! You must all take cover in my cave until Pipsqueak arrives. There is food and drink and time to relax." assured Snowball.

They all followed Snowball into his cosy shelter, leaving his army to stand guard outside. Mia thought Fairy Snow and Icicle would leave, but the two sisters were adamant they would stay until the children reached safety.

"Fairy Snow are we far from the Crystal Kingdom?" enquired Mia.

"You are just a tunnel away," answered Snow mysteriously.

"Does that mean we have to dig our way through?" asked Mia apprehensively. She hated the idea of more setbacks, but perhaps in this strange land, there were dwarves, renowned diggers, who would assist in this physical task.

"No dwarves here!" teased Snow, reading Mia's thoughts.

Snowball was a very gracious host. He ensured everyone was comfortable and well-fed; the jolly fellow even entertained them with a few songs.

"They should nickname you the *singing snowball*," teased Charlie.

"Now don't be a *cheeky* Charlie, or I shall have to reveal your nickname," chuckled Snowball.

"What is it? Please tell us!" interrupted Mia, jumping up and down with excitement.

"It's cheesey," answered Snowball, trying to be more serious but stifling a giggle. "Cheesey Claws!" he added, laughing heartily.

Everyone joined in, even Charlie when Mia pretended to sniff his rather large feet, then pinched her nose in disgust.

For a moment, their troubles were forgotten, when a shout from outside indicated a stranger was approaching. Snowball was quick to respond and told them all to stay inside until the coast was clear. Before he had time to investigate, Pipsqueak came rushing in, clearly out of breath and most distressed.

"Pipsqueak!" everyone shouted, both pleased but alarmed to see that Mistletoe was not with him.

"What's happened? Where is Mistletoe?" questioned Charlie, expecting the worst.

"Here, drink this Pipsqueak and try to calm down," soothed Fairy Snow, who sensed this brave pixie had been through quite an ordeal. She looked at Charlie with a warning to be more sympathetic.

"Okay fella! In your own time," he continued gently, showing more concern.

Pipsqueak began to tell them about the trap Matilda had set to capture Mistletoe, and how he had managed to get away. He was lucky enough to have overheard her plans to meet up with Jack Frost and venture here to stop the children from entering the Crystal Kingdom.

"I'm so sorry I haven't got the magic milk you need," said Pipsqueak dejectedly.

"Don't worry," replied Mia, trying to console Pipsqueak. "I'm sure we can work it out somehow," she comforted him. This was not a time to be despondent; this was a time to believe. "Time!" she cried out.

"Time! Did somebody say Time?" uttered a familiar voice.

Mia spun round, and there hiding behind a tall snowman standing in the far corner of the cave, was her old friend Tick Tock.

"Tick Tock, how good to see you! Can you help us?" asked Mia, wrapping her arms tightly around his small frame.

"Of course! I understand you are only one step away from the Crystal Kingdom, but you haven't succeeded in getting the magic milk to awaken Oakley, and without it, you cannot continue your journey," he acknowledged.

"Yes, that is true," she admitted calmly.

"You need to go back in time. Back to a safer place, where things were more normal. A place and time when Oakley hadn't eaten the berries," he advised.

"I've got it! We need to go back to 'Holly and Ivy's Glen!" she enthused.

"Clever girl! That's right, but it is you, Mia, who must stop Oakley before this event takes place. Do you think you can do it?" he asked.

"I have no other choice and nothing to lose Tick Tock. Please give me back the time I need to do this," she said courageously.

"Unfortunately, *I* am not able to turn the clock back that far Mia, but don't worry, I know somebody who can! Follow me."

Everybody had listened in silence as Mia and Tick Tock spoke. They were all proud of her confidence and determination to free her brother from his deep sleep, regardless of the risk to herself.

Pipsqueak warned them that Matilda and Jack Frost could be close by, so they would have to prepare for battle without further delay. At all costs, they must ensure that Mia had enough time to go back and put things right, so she and Oakley could continue their journey into the Crystal Kingdom.

16. THE CRYSTAL TUNNEL

"Matilda's been spotted Charlie, and I have my men at the ready," reported Snowball.

"Where's Fairy Snow and Icicle?" enquired Charlie.

"Fairy Snow is creating a snowstorm to make visibility poor, but unfortunately, she is up against Blizzard, whipping up the snow against her. It's proving quite an exhaustive battle. Icy is blasting Blizzard with her cold and chilling breath, but Jack Frost is cutting his way through everything," detailed Snowball.

"Doesn't look too good then," interrupted Pipsqueak.

"I'll go and bring the fairies back. It may be more advantageous for them to protect the children," suggested Lightning.

Everyone agreed, and Lightning left the shelter of the cave to go and collect Fairy Snow and Icicle from the battle front. He could see Matilda and her army of gnomes clearly. Jack Frost was at her side with his ice goblins. They were a formidable sight and gaining ground, but Captain Snowball and his men were just as strong and powerful, and Lightning trusted them wholeheartedly to win the day.

It wasn't long before Lightning returned with the fairies. Tick Tock instructed them to stay close to the children and follow him to the 'Crystal Tunnel.' Although their destination was only thirty minutes away, it was important they did not delay. Matilda would be fully aware of what they were trying to achieve, as it was now their only option, and she would be determined to stop it.

It was so very cold and chilling, Mia thought, snuggling deep into Lightning's mane and clutching her brother closely to her.

"It's going to be alright Oakley. You'll soon be awake from the *Land of Nod*," she whispered gently in his ear.

As the snowflakes whirled relentlessly around them, to protect their visibility, the path ahead was not clear, and Mia began to worry that they would never find the tunnel in the storm. Then, she had a brilliant idea, and without a second thought she reached for Twinkle's purse of stars. She gathered a few in her hand and, sitting upright, she tossed them far into the distance. This time they fell to the ground, illuminating the path before them in the snowy darkness.

"Good Thinking Mia," exclaimed Lightning proudly.

"That's okay! I thought it might help us get there quicker if we could see our way more clearly," she replied, feeling a little nervous but excited that if things went to plan, she would not only awaken her brother, but they would be safe in the Crystal Kingdom.

"Oh, I can see him!" interrupted Fairy Snow.

"Me too!" declared Icy.

"Who?" said Mia, squinting her eyes and trying to focus ahead. She couldn't see anything but starlight and snow.

"Tock Tick!" answered Lightning. "We have reached the crystal tunnel Mia."

"Tock Tick! Don't you mean Tick Tock?" queried Mia, thinking maybe he'd left the party and gone on ahead. Suddenly Tick Tock was by her side.

"No Tock Tick Mia! My grandfather, Master of Time and Keeper of Keys," explained Tick Tock, jumping up and down with joy, feeling relieved that they'd reached their destination at last.

As they journeyed forward, Tock Tick became clearer. He was a dwarf-like character who reminded Mia of Father Christmas, with his long beard of white, bushy eyebrows, plump frame and rosy cheeks. Spectacles were perched precariously on the end of his nose, and if he sneezed they would probably fall off! Mia could not believe how little he resembled his grandson, Tick Tock!

"Welcome! Welcome! Welcome!" he jovially repeated, as they all drew to a halt outside the entrance to the tunnel. Mia noticed he was wearing a necklace, like that worn by a mayor, but consisting of many unusual keys of different shapes and sizes. He also carried a huge watch- like sceptre, with the moon and stars etched in gold along its length. His complete attire was that of a wizard; an oversized long cloak, pointed hat and winkle pickers in midnight blue with an astronomical pattern repeated throughout.

Grandfather, we haven't got time today for three-peating!" laughed Tick Tock, embracing his grandfather tenderly.

"Well No no no! Of course not not not!" hiccupped Tock Tick.

Tick Tock turned to Fairy Snow in exasperation. He loved his grandfather dearly, but as he was now getting very old, he tended to repeat the last word of his sentence three times. Although funny, this could be rather annoying, and under the circumstances, time wasting.

Fairy Snow knew only too well what had to be done, and flying to Tock Tick's side, she waved her magical wand over him to freeze the repeated words.

"Step forward Mia" instructed Tock Tick.

"Now listen very carefully! Once you enter the crystal tunnel, with Oakley, I will turn back time and you will see before you, many doorways depicting fragments of your journey so far. One doorway will show your brother about to eat the slumber berries. You must pass through *this* door and stop him! If you can do this, you will have broken the spell. Fail… and there will be no journey forward or back. Do you understand?" emphasized Tock Tick.

"Yes… I understand. There should be no problem. Oakley trusts me, and he will do anything I say! After all, I *am* his *big* sister," replied Mia proudly.
"I know he can be annoying at times, but I do love him, and I want him awake and back with me again," she added.

"One more thing Mia," continued Tock Tick. Mia's heart sank. She knew things were not going to be as easy as she first thought and waited in silence for this educated dwarf's next remark.

112

"Things will not be as you expect. Oakley will not recognise you. You are merely a stranger trying to stop him from doing what he wants to do. He will not want to believe anything you say, and his hunger will cloud his common sense. Do you think you can take on this challenge?"

"I have no choice but to do what is necessary and I will do my best. How much time do I have?" asked Mia.

"You have only the time frame up to the appearance of Holly! Her appearance indicates Oakley has eaten the berries," replied Tock Tick.

Mia fully understood what was expected of her. She must now say goodbye to her friends and take Oakley into the Crystal Tunnel alone. If she succeeded, she would be able to continue her journey through the tunnel into the Crystal Kingdom, where they would finally be safe from Queen Matilda. She didn't bear think of the consequences of failure. Clutching Bluebell's crystal protectively, and carrying the few remaining stars in Twinkle's purse, she followed Lightning into the tunnel where Oakley was left with her.

"Good Luck Mia" whispered Lightning. "We'll all be waiting for you!" she reassured her.

"I really do hope so…!" she sighed, as a small tear escaped from the corner of her eye.

She turned to see if Lightning had noticed, but she was gone.

17. BREAKING THE SPELL

Mia stood in the tunnel, with Oakley lying at her feet still unconscious. The silence was overwhelming and spooky, the coldness seeping into her bones. Suddenly, a light surrounded her, and a series of doorways appeared in the walls either side. It was time to go back in time and find the relevant event, which would save her brother from an eternity of sleep. She had been told there was no need to take Oakley with her, so she made sure he was comfortable under the warmth of Ivy's jacket and pulled her garment closer to her.

She proceeded along a corridor, peering in through each doorway. She was amazed to see the calendar of events they had both shared, beginning with the discovery of Bluebell.

When she reached door number 8, she could see from within, that Pipsqueak had just made his catastrophic entrance into the Glen of Holly and Ivy, much to the delight of one of the woodland nymphs. It was strange to see herself in this time frame, and she knew she must hide her appearance, as she could confuse herself and maybe alienate her brother further. When she entered the portal, she would be a stranger to Oakley, not his beloved sister. It was all so very complicated.

She continued to watch the drama unfold and just as Oakley saw the red berries gleaming on the bush and started to make his way over to eat them, she dived through the doorway and landed on top of him. It was with expertise that she kept him pinned to the ground, so he was hidden from anyone's view in the grass.

"Get off me!" he began to shout.

"Ssh! Ssh!" whispered Mia, putting her finger to her lips and winking.

He would have cried out again, but for a brief second, he looked at Mia. He didn't know this strange girl, but for some reason he thought he did. It must be the twinkle in her eyes, almost familiar.

"Who are you?" he asked inquisitively, keeping his voice low as he knew his sister was not far away, and he wanted to keep his strange friend a secret for now.

"I am a friend of Bluebell's," replied Mia, thinking on the spot. She knew this statement would at least reassure Oakley of her good intentions, but her brother was not as stupid as she would have liked him to be on this occasion.

"Prove it!" he ordered, raising his voice slightly.

"Here! I have her crystal," she said, taking the blue gem out of her pocket.

Oakley reached forward and grabbed the crystal from her hand.

"You are nothing but a fraud and a thief," he yelled at the top of his voice. "My sister is the only one who holds Bluebell's crystal, and you must have stolen it from her."

Mia…Mia! Come over here quickly!" he screamed.

"Please Oakley, believe me! I have a crystal too, and I have come to warn you not to eat those berries. I know you are hungry, but you must wait."

She was about to warn him of the berries' curse, but as she looked up, she saw herself come running towards them. She knew she had to get away and not face herself. As she ran towards the doorway and exited back into the time tunnel, she hoped she had done enough to break the spell.

She felt so drained emotionally and physically, that she laid herself down on the cold snowy ground and silently began to cry.

"Mia…Wake up! What are you crying for?" consoled Oakley, thinking his sister was having a bad dream.

"I am awake!" declared Mia, "And I am crying for you Oakley."

Oakley thought his sister had gone crazy, so he decided to shake her; with little response he gathered up the snow around them and sprinkled it in her hair. He was just about to rub some in her face when she jumped up unexpectedly.

"Oakley…? You're awake" she proclaimed joyously, smothering him with 'girly' kisses.

"That's enough Mia! What's wrong with you?" he asked, feeling baffled by his sister's actions.

116

"There is no time to explain Oakley!" she continued, gaining her composure.

Mia was overwhelmed with the success of her mission and couldn't quite believe her brother was back to his normal self. She had no time to tell him of their previous adventures, as she knew they were not safe until they reached the Crystal Kingdom.

"Where are we?" enquired Oakley. The last memory he had was being pinned down by a strange girl who had stolen Bluebell's crystal. She was telling him not to eat the berries, as she ran from him and then suddenly disappeared.

"There is no time to explain Oakley," she repeated, raising her voice.

"It is not safe to stay here!" she emphasised.

"Where are we going then?" asked Oakley, clearly not remembering anything.

Mia looked around her and felt rather confused and upset that nobody was there to escort them to safety. It didn't seem that long since she had passed through the time portal, yet everyone had disappeared and now she was alone with her brother. What had happened to her close friends?

She had no time to worry, she must take immediate action. Turning her attention to Oakley, she answered him with a confidence she didn't really feel.

"We have to make our way to the Crystal Kingdom, which I think is at the end of this tunnel."

She couldn't remember anyone giving her directions, so assumed the way was forward.

Oakley looked at his sister, and lines of worry began to etch on his face. Seeing his concern, Mia automatically wrapped her arms around him in reassurance.

"Don't worry Oakley! We will soon be safe and sound, I promise. Just keep close and follow me," she comforted him.

Trustingly, Oakley grabbed his sister's hand, as together they made their way through the cold dark tunnel, with a crisp carpet of white snow beneath their feet, illuminating the way. Hopefully, this would lead them to safety and their journey's end.

18. THE VOICE

They had been walking endlessly through the tunnel, the cold and fatigue seeping into their bones with each step. Mia was growing frustrated and Oakley became impatient and irritated.

"How much further Mia?" he whined, for the umpteenth time.

"Are you even sure we're going the right way?" he questioned constantly.

"Stop worrying Oakley! I'm certain the way is forward," she told him, trying to sound more positive than she felt. It was becoming increasingly difficult not to lose her temper, and it made her realise how patient her parents were at similar times.

"Forward…Forward…Forward" repeated a voice out of the blue. Mia became excited. Was that a familiar voice she heard behind her?

"Is that you Tock Tick?" asked Mia, feeling a little relieved and grateful that at least somebody had stayed behind to wait for them.

"Tock Tick…. Tock Tick…. Tock Tick," replied the unseen voice.

"We can't see you Tock Tick, but can you tell us in which direction we have to go?" she enquired. They needed to keep moving as she did not know how far away Matilda and her

JOURNEY TO THE CRYSTAL KINGDOM

army were. She hoped Captain Snowball was still holding her back, but she could not be sure.

"Backwards......Backwards......Backwards...... Backwards," instructed the voice, cutting through the darkness.

Instantly Mia's suspicion was aroused. Tock Tick only repeated the last word of his sentence three times, and now he was telling her to go backwards; she felt very confused. Tock Tick would not mislead her, so who possessed this mystery voice? Now was the time for smart thinking, in case it was a trap.

After exiting doorway number 8, Mia had felt very disorientated and wasn't quite sure in which direction to go. It seemed sensible to move forward. She couldn't waste any more time playing games with the voice, she had to know whether it was friend or foe! Perhaps she could trick the *magical being*. It was worth a try...

Oakley had other ideas. He was more inquisitive and wanted to know who was messing around with them. Slowly, he ventured away from Mia while she was deep in thought. He was the master of hide n' seek and loved to play the detective. He knew his sister would have stopped him if he had outlined his plan, so he crept along the tunnel in the direction of the voice without her.

"Tell me Tock Tick, why do you now suggest going backwards?" she questioned.

"Backwards!" confirmed the voice once again.

Mia was growing tired of this charade. She was going to get to the bottom of this matter once and for all!

"You are not Tock Tick!" shouted Mia. "Who are you?" she demanded.

"You…. You…. You!" repeated the voice.

"Enough of this nonsense! I am Mia!" she yelled back angrily.

"Mia! Mia! I have found him!" she heard Oakley cry from deep within the tunnel.

For a minute she thought she was still being duped, until she turned to her side and realised Oakley was no longer there. Immediately she became very frightened and anxious, as she knew her little brother was in danger yet again. There was only one thing she could think to do, so she reached for the tiny crystal in her pocket to summon the help of Bluebell.

"Oh no!" she gasped in despair. It was no longer there! Where was it? Somehow, she couldn't remember!

"Come back here Oakley! she yelled at the top of her voice.

Although Oakley had heard Mia loud and clear, he did not move. He was more interested in the little elf that was sitting on a rock in front of him, with a giant mirror held upright in his tiny hand. He seemed to be admiring his reflection. Suddenly he turned to Oakley, and smiling with an evil toothless grin, he introduced himself.

"Well hello boy! I am glad you have decided to join me. I am

Eduardo Echo. My friends call me Eddy, my enemies Echo, the choice is yours!"

"I am definitely not your friend and I will not be joining you. I have just come to find out who is playing tricks on me and my sister," said Oakley defiantly.

"Why! You are quite a fire cracker when you are awake, but your bravado is wasted on me," he cackled like a hagged witch.

Oakley was not frightened by this ugly looking elf, with his long straggly hair, slanted eyes of steel, and small hooked nose. He found him rather amusing, and would've continued to talk with him further, but the feeling that this wouldn't be wise, made him head back towards his sister, as she had instructed.

"Wait Oakley! Don't go! Your sister is coming to join you here." he called out temptingly.

"How can I trust you?" asked Oakley, stopping in his tracks and turning to face Echo.

"Come here and take a look in my mirror and you will see your sister clearly making her way towards us," replied the mischievous elf, enticing him back.

Echo held the mirror outstretched in his tiny hand, his long twig like fingers gripping the handle, and Oakley could see from where he stood, the image of his sister running as fast as she could towards them.

Although it seemed Echo was indeed being helpful, Oakley still did not trust him and decided it was best to keep some distance from him, until Mia arrived safely. Then they would both decide what to do next.

Echo was not a bit concerned about the boy being cautious. Under the circumstances it was to be expected. He was very excited that his scheme was going to plan and knew he would be greatly rewarded for the capture of these 'most wanted' children. His name would go down in history, and perhaps he would receive a medal.

Grinning to himself, he knew it was only a matter of time before Matilda joined them, and his task was fulfilled. He had to admit he rather liked the boy's defiance, but sentiments were not allowed when a kingdom was at stake.

He was disturbed from his reverie, when Mia came charging in. Grabbing Oakley, she pulled him back abruptly and told him to run with her, as fast as he could, away from the cunning elf.

"Wait…I can help you!" called Echo, as they were about to turn around the corner and out of sight.

Oakley pulled at his sister's arm this time.

"Let's just listen to what he has to say Mia. After all, we don't really know which way we have to go to get to the Crystal Kingdom." he pointed out.

Mia decided Oakley was right, maybe Echo could help them. Maybe she was misjudging him. No harm had come to her brother, so perhaps she should give him the benefit of the doubt. They slowly made their way over to Echo, but before reaching him, Mia suddenly noticed a shadow lurking in the tunnel behind him. A distinctive crown upon the bearer's head could only mean one thing...Queen Matilda!

"Run Oakley, run!" screamed Mia, pushing her brother so hard he nearly fell over.

"It's a trap! It's Matilda!" she shrieked.

As they ran through the tunnel, their hearts racing, they could hear Matilda not far behind them, screaming her orders.

"Get the little brats! Catch them! Don't let them escape, or there *will* be a price to pay!" she bellowed, her voice more colder and chilling than the tunnel itself.

19. THE ARRIVAL

Frightened and exhausted, they couldn't run any further. Mia began to cry, convinced there was no way out. They didn't know which way to go to reach safety; Matilda would soon capture them. If only she hadn't lost Bluebell's crystal.

"Don't cry Mia, I'm here," said Oakley bravely. He cradled his sister in his arms with a strong sense of protection. This made her cry even more, realising how much her brother cared for, and loved, her.

"Here, take my handkerchief and dry your eyes," he suggested kindly, withdrawing the small white tissue from his pocket and handing it to her. To her surprise, as she unraveled it carefully, there fell upon her lap, the tiny blue crystal. At once she remembered what had happened and, turning to Oakley, she explained.

"Of course! You snatched it from me, in the glen, when I went back in time to save you," she laughed, feeling so relieved that she hadn't lost it after all.

"We also have Twinkle's magic stars," she reassured him. "In all the confusion I must have forgotten about them too."

Oakley didn't fully understand how this gem was going to defend them against Matilda, or what the stars could do, but his sister seemed hopeful.

Mia knew there was no time to waste. She withdrew two stars

from the purse in her pocket, and threw one in front of her, and one behind. Immediately, the path ahead became brightly lit, but behind was only darkness.

"We *are* going in the right direction," cried Oakley.

"It looks like it," replied Mia, feeling more confident and positive.

"It looks like it...it...it...it!" echoed a voice.

"Oh no!" cried Oakley in anguish, turning around to face Eduardo Echo. He was holding his mirror aloft, showing their images. It was evident he had been following them, and there was no way of escaping him now. There was only one other thing they could do!

"Mia, the crystal!" instructed Oakley.

"Please help us Bluebell! We need your magic to protect us and bring us safely home," called out his sister, clutching the stone closely to her heart.

Instantly, an icy chill enveloped their surroundings. Could this suggest Jack Frost's ominous presence?

As they held their breath, a familiar fairy known to Mia, appeared in front of them. Her face was etched with anger, and Oakley now huddled closer to his sister, not knowing what to expect.

"Don't be afraid Oakley! She is on *our* side," she consoled him.

"Stand back children," warned Icy, as she began to blow a cold sharp frost in the direction of Echo. His evil grin dissipated, and he fell silent. Shivering and shaking before them, he could no longer hold his magic mirror. Finally, it shattered into pieces and fell to the ground. Realising he was beaten, it was time for him to make his escape before he froze completely, becoming no more than a statue of ice.

As Echo retreated into the darkness, Icy turned to the children and smiled affectionately.

"Quickly children, it's time to go," she urged. "Although I've broken Matilda's communication with the mirror that Echo held to show your location, I sense she is still looking for you. Therefore, you must follow the stars which will lead you to the 'Crystal Kingdom,' and safety.

"But what about you Icy? We cannot leave you here, to face Matilda alone," said Mia anxiously.

"I will be fine! My icy breath will chill them all to the bones and stop their advance whilst you get away. Now hurry! I will see you in the kingdom," she ordered. Seconds later she had disappeared in the same direction as Echo.

The children now looked to the few stars they had scattered in front of them and began to follow the illuminated pathway. As they ventured on, the stars began to multiply, appearing on both sides of the tunnel and overhead. It felt as though they were in a kaleidoscope, everything seemed to be moving, making them feel lightheaded and dizzy.

"I think I'm going to be sick," moaned Oakley.

"Me too!" replied Mia, hoping they would soon be at their

destination. She prayed this was not another trap, as it seemed they had been walking for ages.

Suddenly, their thoughts were shattered by a bolt of brilliant golden light, which engulfed the tunnel, splintering the stars into a cascade of tiny silver fragments. They looked down, shielding their eyes from the brightness. Their bodies relaxed in the warmth of the glow emanating around them, and their sickness now forgotten, they moved effortlessly on. A familiar voice broke the silence.

"Welcome Children! You're safe at last!" declared Charlie happily.

As they looked up, they were amazed by the beauty of the landscape before them. Multi-coloured crystals embellished the scenery. A spectacular diamond quartz castle towered on a hill in front of them. The crystal structure shimmered in the sunlight, casting radiant beams far and wide. The children were uplifted by such a view.

"The Crystal Kingdom," they exclaimed in awe. A huge sense of relief overwhelmed them, as they recognized the familiar faces gathered around. It was such a wonderful feeling.

"Congratulations children! You're finally here. Now it is time to meet your Queen," announced Bluebell, hovering excitedly in front of them.

"Escort at the ready Miss," chuckled Charlie, perching himself on top of Mia's shoulder.

"Glad to see you're finally awake Son!" he added, looking down at Oakley affectionately.

Lightning and Pipsqueak smiled with pride. It was good to see everyone happy and having fun again. The children certainly deserved it after the long and dangerous journey they had encountered. But little did they know that their quest had only just begun...

ABOUT THE AUTHOR

J.A. (Jacqueline Ann) Kefford always had a wild imagination as a child, believing in fairies and magic. At the age of 11, she began writing short stories, which her sisters would often sit and listen to, before going to bed. Over the years, she has worked as a secretary, P.A, and book keeper.

Jacqui loves singing, dancing and acting, and belongs to a local choir and amateur dramatic society. She is also a keen gardener, has a passion for a variety of music, art and craftwork, and believes in the power of crystals!

With retirement looming, she suffered a bout of depression, but out of the blue, had the idea to write this novel. Her belief in fairies and magic made writing this book a labour of love, and Jacqui hopes both children and adults will enjoy the first of the trilogy of this fantasy adventure.

To contact: mamajaks56@gmail.com

Made in the USA
Columbia, SC
26 November 2018